DREAD LOCKS

NEAL SHUSTERMAN

darkfusion ▲ BOOK 1

DREAD LOCKS

DUTTON CHILDREN'S BOOKS ▲ NEW YORK

DUTTON CHILDREN'S BOOKS

A division of Penguin Young Readers Group
Published by the Penguin Group
Penguin Group (USA) Inc., 375 Hudson Street, New York, New York 10014, U.S.A.
Penguin Group (Canada), 10 Alcorn Avenue, Toronto, Ontario, Canada M4V 3B2
(a division of Pearson Penguin Canada Inc.)
Penguin Books Ltd, 80 Strand, London WC2R 0RL, England
Penguin Ireland, 25 St Stephen's Green, Dublin 2, Ireland (a division of Penguin Books Ltd)
Penguin Group (Australia), 250 Camberwell Road, Camberwell, Victoria 3124, Australia
(a division of Pearson Australia Group Pty Ltd)
Penguin Books India Pvt Ltd, 11 Community Centre, Panchsheel Park, New Delhi - 110 017, India
Penguin Group (NZ), Cnr Airborne and Rosedale Roads, Albany, Auckland 1310, New Zealand
(a division of Pearson New Zealand Ltd)
Penguin Books (South Africa) (Pty) Ltd, 24 Sturdee Avenue,
Rosebank, Johannesburg 2196, South Africa
Penguin Books Ltd, Registered Offices: 80 Strand, London WC2R 0RL, England

This book is a work of fiction. Names, characters, places, and incidents are either the product of
the author's imagination or are used fictitiously, and any resemblance to actual persons, living or
dead, business establishments, events, or locales is entirely coincidental.

LIBRARY OF CONGRESS CATALOGING-IN-PUBLICATION DATA

Shusterman, Neal.
Dread locks/by Neal Shusterman.—1st ed.
p. cm.
Summary: Accustomed to a carefree existence, fifteen-year-old Parker Baer meets the girl next
door and finds his life taking a menacing turn as he begins to absorb some of her terrible powers.
ISBN 0-525-47554-0
[1. Fear—Fiction. 2. Friendship—Fiction. 3. Family life—Fiction. 4. Schools—Fiction.
5. Supernatural—Fiction.] I. Title.
PZ7.S55987Dr 2005
[Fic]—dc22   2004022065

Published in the United States by Dutton Children's Books,
a division of Penguin Young Readers Group
345 Hudson Street, New York, New York 10014
www.penguin.com/youngreaders

Designed by Jason Henry

Printed in USA ▴ First Edition
1 3 5 7 9 10 2 6 4 2

For Eric and Jan,
may your midnight buffet plate always be full

———————

ACKNOWLEDGMENTS

▲

Dread Locks would not have been possible without the support and contributions of quite a few people:

Eric Elfman, whose crucial creative input helped to mold many key chapters; Jean Feiwel, for giving me the first shot with this story; Tonya Martin, for her insightful early editorial work; Easton Royce, for knowing when it's time for a pseudonym to go away; Andrea Brown, for believing in the *Dark Fusion* series and bringing it to my market; my assistant, Janine Black, for her tireless efforts running interference and keeping me on task; my kids, who have become so good at critiquing stories, it's scary.

And finally, Stephanie Owens Lurie, who has shepherded me from the very beginning of my career. I couldn't hope for a better editor or friend.

▼

DREAD LOCKS

I've been thinking about it a lot. It seems all I can do these days is think, playing the events over and over again in my mind until I'm numb. I see all the ways it could have turned out differently. How the nightmare could have been avoided, and the deaths—all the deaths—would never have happened.

You have to understand I never intended to be a part of Tara's cruelty. I just couldn't help myself. I couldn't resist, and if you knew her, you wouldn't be able to resist either. I have to believe that it wasn't just my weakness, but a power dark and devious, as irresistible as gravity. I have to believe that, or I'll lose my mind. I can't lose that, you see—it's the only thing I have left...

1

MY LIFE as a STATUE

There was never anything wrong with my life. Perhaps that was the problem. That was the flaw—the crack into which Tara slid like rainwater into a sidewalk fracture, freezing and thawing again and again, widening the crack with each frost. The crack in my life was the fact that I had everything I wanted, or could ever want—and when you have it all, boredom grows like a fungus, coating everything you own and everything you feel.

"You're just a spoiled brat," my older brother, Garrett, would tell me. Him, with his Rolex watch and his designer clothes. Him, with a Lexus in the driveway for his sixteenth birthday. The sad thing is, he was right. By the time I was fourteen, I had a DVD collection that would rival the neighborhood video store. I had three bikes: mountain, racing, and trick. And I knew that whether I wanted one or not, there would be a Lexus in the driveway for me one day, too.

No, there was nothing wrong with my life. But then again, everything was wrong.

On my fifteenth birthday, I came to realize that the expression *spoiled rotten* meant exactly that. We kids were the apples of our parents' eyes, and I, for one, was rotting from the inside out.

I was looking forward to my birthday—I mean, who doesn't. That was when I cared what I would get. That was when I cared, period. I came running down the stairs that morning, like it was Christmas. My parents were already up. In my family, presents never waited; they were there upon waking. Our family has a problem with what they call delayed gratification. We want *what* we want *when* we want it, and we always want it *now*. So birthday presents never waited until afternoon, or even until after breakfast.

The gift was hard to miss. It was this huge box almost four feet tall and wrapped with a giant red ribbon, sitting smack in the middle of the living room.

"Mine, mine, mine!" yelled my little sister, Katrina. Everything was hers, hers, hers. She was eight, but got attention by acting like she was four.

"Katrina, it's Parker's birthday, not yours," Mom said patiently.

"It's bigger than my present was," Katrina complained, "and don't tell me that size doesn't matter, because you got mad at Dad that time your anniversary diamond was too small."

Dad chuckled uncomfortably. Mom sighed.

"Maybe you'll get something as big for your next birthday," Dad offered.

"Christmas," demanded Katrina. "Christmas is sooner."

Garrett, whose bed hair looked like something out of a bad science-fiction movie, threw up his hands like my birthday was an imposition on his life. "Can we just get on with this already?"

I looked at the box on the table, trying to take it slow, relishing the mystery. I had no idea what it was. I had dropped hints that I wanted a motocross bike, but this box wasn't the right shape.

"Go on, open it," said Dad.

I tugged the end of the huge ribbon like a rip cord, and the bow pulled open. As it did, the sides of the box, which weren't actually attached, fell away to reveal a metallic shape inside. It took a moment to realize what it was.

It was me.

"Well, what do you think?" asked Mom.

What did I think? I wasn't quite thinking yet—I was still trying to take it in. It was a three-foot bronze sculpture of me holding a basketball, ready to shoot. The thing looked like the top of a giant trophy—like the MVP trophy I had gotten on my basketball team the year before, but with my face.

"It's something, isn't it!" Dad said proudly.

"I don't play basketball anymore," I reminded them.

Dad threw me an irritated glare. "You did when we commissioned the artist to sculpt it."

"This year we thought we'd get you something that would last," Mom said. "Something you could pass on to your children."

I had no idea why my future children would want a sculpture of me shooting hoops. What do you say to a present like that?

"Cool," I said.

My parents seemed satisfied with my response.

"Enough of this garbage," said Garrett. "Go out on the driveway—my present to you is there."

"It's a motocross bike," said Katrina, thrilled by her own power to ruin the surprise.

As it was Saturday, I filled the motocross bike with gas, spent the whole day riding until I got bored with it, then took it on tour to all of my friends, until I got bored with that, too.

That night was the first time I truly began to understand how I was rotting from the inside. After dark, I sat in the backyard staring at that bronze sculpture. My parents had already placed it on a pedestal, with lights shining at it from two different angles, and I thought how strange it all was. I had everything that I needed, everything that I wanted, and on top of all that, I now had a statue to honor me. This was as good as it gets. Which meant the only direction from here would be down.

I don't expect you to understand. *Boo hoo, the rich kid's feeling sorry for himself.* But it's not like that. I mean, we're all striving for something, right? There's always something we're working toward. You take that lousy summer job because it gives you the money to actually do something with your friends other than hang out. You dress cool to be in with the popular kids. You bust your butt so that your grades get you to the top of your class. You play basketball dreaming of victory and the MVP trophy.

But what happens when you've got all those things already? What is there to strive for? What do you hope for?

It was as I stared at my own bronze face, feeling that boredom fungus growing all around me, that I heard the first moving van pull up the long driveway of the house next door.

2

THIrTeen MOVING VanS

The place next door had been deserted for as long as I can remember and is the largest house in the neighborhood, if one could actually call it a house. Our place is not quite a mansion, but it comes close. Six bedrooms, a four-car garage, a "bonus room" large enough for both a pool table and a Ping-Pong table, and a yard with a tennis court and pool. The place next door, though, hidden behind ancient sycamore trees, at the end of a gated driveway, was like its own universe. It stood three stories tall, with a winding staircase you could see through the bare front windows. From the outside it looked kind of like the White House, but it was painted canary yellow, which was peeling to reveal the aging wood beneath. The place was so run-down because no one had lived there since before I was born.

My friends and I went there once in a while to look into the dust-covered windows.

"The place is haunted," my best friend, Danté, once told me.

His real name is Don Taylor, which became Don Tay and finally Danté, because he decided that spelling was so much cooler.

"People say every empty old house is haunted," I answered.

"Ralphy Sherman says the guy who lived there hacked off his own head, then went around headless, hacking off the heads of his whole family."

"Ralphy Sherman also says he was JFK in a previous life. You gonna believe that?"

Haunted or not, the place had always had a heavy padlock on the driveway gate. Now either someone had finally bought it, or the original owners were finally moving in after all those years.

I watched from my bedroom window that night, trying to get a glimpse through the trees to see what was going on. Even my parents were curious—I could hear them in their bedroom muttering nightmare neighbor stories to each other and hoping we wouldn't have one of our own. I counted thirteen huge moving vans pulling into the long driveway before I fell asleep.

The next morning—Sunday—while everyone else slept late, I went out to explore.

I rode my new motorbike past the rusty front gate of the mansion a few times. The chain and padlock were gone, but the gate was still closed. It wasn't exactly an invitation to visit, but I'm not one to wait for invitations. I hid my bike in the bushes and climbed through a gap in the fence farther up the road so I'd be less obvious.

When I got to the house, I could see that the vans were all gone. The only sign that the movers had been there were dusty footprints on the porch. I dared to peer inside. The place was still a wreck, but now it was filled with luxurious furniture. Old stuff—the kind they put in fake rooms in museums, then block off with red velvet ropes. Bubble-wrapped artwork leaned against the peeling walls everywhere, and boxes were stacked like building blocks halfway to the vaulted ceiling. Whoever had moved in was probably asleep after such a long night of moving. I sneaked around to the back and peered in to find more of the same in the kitchen and dining room. I didn't dare try the back doorknob, because I didn't want to be tempted to go in.

Cutting through the trees, I climbed back out to the road the way I had come, took my bike on a nice long ride, then went home.

When I got back, Dad was awake, and he was crankier than his usual pre-coffee crank. "What were you doing in my office?" Dad asked me, as if I was guilty of some federal offense.

"I wasn't in your office," I told him. "I was out riding."

"Then one of you is lying."

He led me into his home office, a room that seemed entirely carved out of dark cherrywood, even the floor and desk. Garrett and Katrina were already there, annoyed at this ongoing investigation. Dad pointed to his leather desk chair.

"Someone's been sitting in my chair!" he said.

Garrett rubbed his eyes to get the sleep out of them. "What's the big deal?"

"In case you've forgotten, this is not just a chair, it's an ergonomical skeletal support system." He pointed to four electric buttons that worked like the controls on car seats. "The settings are all off. It took me weeks to get them just right."

"Maybe you did it yourself," I suggested.

"Oh please," he said, disgusted, as if he'd never be capable of such an act.

"What's a *herbo-comical skeleton*," Katrina asked, with worry in her voice. "Is there one in the house? Does it have to stay here?"

"Don't worry about it," I told her. "It doesn't come out until dark."

Katrina bit her lip, and Dad forced me to explain that there was no skeleton; all it meant was that the chair was specially designed for Dad's back problems.

"Actually, all it really means," Garrett said, "is that they overcharged Dad for the chair."

After an uncomfortable silence, I asked, "Can we go now?"

Dad looked at us suspiciously, then waved his hand. "Just don't touch my chair again."

As it turned out, unauthorized chair use was not the only crime of the day. At the breakfast table, Mom handed Katrina her box of cereal. Mom had given up on trying to get Katrina to drink milk—which she hated—and even had given up on making Katrina eat out of a bowl. The best she could do was get Katrina to wash her hands before sitting at the table, where she would shove those grubby little fingers into the cereal box.

"Hey," she said, when she dipped her hand into the box. "Someone's been eating my cereal!"

I shoveled in spoonfuls of my own Wheaties. "I don't think

anyone else in this house can stomach Sugar-Frosted Pizza Puffs," I said. "Your cereal's safe."

"It wasn't even open yesterday, and now half of it's gone!" She dug her hand deep into the box, spilling the awful tomato-colored puffs all over the table. "The prize! Someone took the prize!"

"Honey," said Mom, "maybe they just forgot to put one in."

"Mom, it's a *company.* They would never forget an important thing like that. They could lose their license or something."

Katrina grumbled about her missing cereal prize for the rest of breakfast, making the meal even more unpleasant than usual.

While Dad fine-tuned the adjustments on his chair, and Katrina nagged Mom for a new box of cereal, I went up to my room to plan my day. Mom would want us to go to church, but if Garrett and I did some tag-team stalling, we'd be too late to go. I could head down to the mall, meet up with Danté, maybe catch a movie or something. Same old thing every week. I was about to sit at my desk when I happened to catch sight of something in the room, and what I saw made me freak. You know that feeling you get when your leg falls asleep? Well, I suddenly had that feeling in my spine. Like termites were chewing through the marrow in my backbone. I tore out of the room and downstairs, finding Dad just finishing up his chair adjustments. He must have caught the look on my face.

"What's up, Parker?"

"Dad . . . someone's sleeping in my bed."

3

▲

THE someone
sleepinG in MY BeD

You might think such a thing as someone sleeping in your bed wouldn't be the cause of a major freaking—but if you think that, then it's never happened to you. The fact was, everyone in my house was accounted for. My brother, my sister, my parents. It couldn't be our cat, Nasdaq—he was much smaller than the lump in my bed. That meant whoever was in that bed was an intruder.

Dad and I went up—Dad carrying the trusty tire iron that he kept in the house in case of a break-in. "I think it's a bum, or something," I told him. "Some crazy bum who climbed in through a window. He could be dangerous."

"We'll see."

We slowly entered my room, and Dad stiffened. Maybe he had thought it was my imagination, but now he knew it was not. A hand stuck out from beneath my covers. We approached the figure in the bed. What if he had a knife—or worse, a gun? My heart drummed against my chest like a low-dribbled basketball.

I reached out, clasped the quilt in my hand, and pulled the covers from the intruder's face.

The intruder was a girl.

She slept soundly, the morning sun shining through the blinds onto her face. Even sleeping, I could tell she was pretty. No, not so much pretty as exotic. Her face was so unique it defined its own beauty.

Dad lowered his tire iron. "You know her?"

I shook my head. She seemed about my age, but I didn't recognize her from school. Her hair was the most interesting thing about her. Her head was covered with long, looping curls—bright golden twists of hair tumbling in all directions on my pillow. They were almost like dreadlocks, but very different in the way they glowed, catching the light in glimmering spirals that made each blond curl seem almost alive. I had never seen anything like it.

I reached out and poked her shoulder. She stirred slightly. I prodded her again. "Hey, wake up."

She rolled over, away from us, and pulled up something that had been hidden under the covers. I gasped, thinking it was a weapon—but it was just a pair of sunglasses. She slipped them on, then turned back to us.

"Good morning!" she said, stretching like a cat. I immediately caught the English accent in her voice.

"Do you mind telling me what you're doing in my son's bed?"

"I can handle this, Dad." I looked sternly at her reflective glasses. "Do you mind telling me what you're doing in my bed?"

She laughed. "Well, all the other beds in your house weren't as comfortable as yours."

That just made Dad stammer, then state the obvious: "This isn't your house!"

"So?"

"How long have you been here?" I asked her.

She grinned at me. "Since you went over to my house to peek in the windows."

Now it was my turn to stammer. I'm sure I also turned red. Dad looked from me, to her, and back to me again.

"I . . . I was just checking out the new neighbors," I told Dad, then turned back to the girl. "So *you* moved in next door?"

She held out her hand for me to shake. "My name's Tara. Tara Herpecheveux."

I almost laughed. "That's a mouthful."

"It's French."

Hmm, I thought. *English accent, French name.* She was already more interesting than anyone else I knew. "I'm Parker." I shook her hand, all the while thinking how weird it was to be introducing myself to some girl in my bed while my father stood next to me with a tire iron.

"Parker Merritt Baer," she said.

I was genuinely surprised. "You know me?"

"I saw your name on the trophies." She pointed to my trophy shelf across the room. For some reason I was glad she had taken the time to notice them before taking a nap.

"This is a strange way to introduce yourself, Miss Herpecheveux," my father said.

"But memorable," she answered. "Bet you'll never forget meeting me!"

She pulled back the covers all the way, to reveal that she was wearing a flowery summer dress, even though it was fall, and the leaves were already beginning to turn. She was barefoot, and her toenails were painted a curious granite gray. Although I hadn't noticed it before, so were her fingernails.

We saw her to the front door.

"You have a beautiful home," she said as she stepped out. "I especially like your collection of sculpted glass."

That meant she had been in the den, where Mom kept all the shapeless glass artworks she buys. I wondered how much of the house Tara had explored before commandeering my bed—and how she could have been so stealthy that no one noticed her.

"We do have a security system," Dad told her. "You were lucky it wasn't set."

She only smiled, and Dad walked off, satisfied that she was on the other side of the front-door threshold. But I held the door open.

"Well," I said, "welcome to the neighborhood . . . I think."

And then she asked me something. "When you came over to my house, why didn't you come in? The door was open."

"Because there's a little felony called trespassing," I said.

"Simple trespassing is not a felony—it's a misdemeanor."

"Whatever it is, it's still not right. I wouldn't just walk into your house uninvited."

She raised an eyebrow. "Maybe next time you should."

I closed the door, but her silhouette against the bright morning remained like a shadow on my vision long after she was gone.

4

▲

TOO COOL FOR
THE SCHOOL

Although I didn't see Tara again for the rest of the day, I couldn't get her out of my mind. That night I was half-hoping she'd appear, uninvited, in our house again—maybe grab a soda out of the refrigerator and watch the big-screen TV in the family room.

No such luck.

"We should have been nicer to her," I told my father at dinner. "We scared her away."

Dad laughed at that. "I didn't exactly see her running away from us in terror."

He was right. To be honest, I had been the only one terrified when I had seen there was someone hidden under my covers. And even though she strode off with a rare kind of confidence, I found myself really wondering when I'd see her again and wondering why I cared.

Monday morning, for the first time in a long time, I looked forward to going to school. I hoped Tara's parents had decided to send her to the same fancy private school I was in. The Excelsior Academy. With the school's tall gates and thick, ivy-covered stone walls, our parents had the satisfaction of knowing their precious darlings were protected from the real world. Or so they thought.

Sure enough, as soon as I entered the school grounds, I saw her.

Tara was standing just inside the gate, leaning against the wall, watching as the other students streamed in. It looked like she was doing a head count while at the same time boldly announcing her presence among us. Or maybe she was just trying to familiarize herself with the faces of her new peers.

"Hi," I said, stopping in front of her.

"Hey, there, Baby Baer," said Tara.

It should have made me angry, but it didn't. "Technically speaking, my sister's the youngest in the family, so *she'd* be Baby Baer."

"Naah," said Tara. "She's Little Miss Muffett." Which was true enough, because Katrina was deathly afraid of spiders.

Tara had on her reflective sunglasses. Her blond curls tumbled and twitched around her shoulders, glowing in the bright morning light. She wore an elegantly woven Japanese jacket of shiny black satin over a cream-colored silk shirt tucked into camouflage paratrooper pants.

I had never seen anyone like her before, and apparently neither had anyone else. Everyone was checking her out as they entered through the gate—guys, girls, even the teachers. It would have been hard to miss her. Standing there in the courtyard, she was as out of place as a Siberian tiger on the school's front lawn.

It was funny watching the reactions of the other kids as they made their way past her. Most of them tried to get a good look while pretending she was no big deal, but no one dared to talk to her—they were too intimidated by her sheer presence and confidence. Not even Ernest Benson, the school's top jock, would approach. He just paused to goggle at her—which didn't make his girlfriend, Melanie, very happy.

As for Tara, it seemed as if, behind her sunglasses, her eyes were flicking over every person who walked through the gate, sizing them up, deciding if they were worthy. Worthy of what, I had no idea.

"Do you know where your first class is?" I asked her.

"I've got it," she said, not looking at me. A busload of kids had just been dropped off at the curb. They were all entering at once, and she didn't want to miss any of them. "I'm all set."

"I could walk you to—"

"I've got it," she repeated, more emphatically. But then she turned to me and smiled. "Thank you."

I nodded and backed away, not quite willing to take my eyes off her until I had to. Finally, I turned and passed under the stone-arch entrance of the school.

Danté was waiting inside for me with one of my other friends, Freddy Furbush, famous schoolwide for being able to let loose ear-deafening burps on command.

"Who—was—that?" Danté demanded, emphasizing every word.

"And what were *you* doing talking to her?" asked Freddy, in awe.

"She's my new neighbor." I tried to sound casual but didn't quite pull it off. "I met her yesterday, when she moved in." I didn't mention the part about exactly *how* I had met her. "She came over for a visit."

"I'm gonna be spending a lot more time at your house," said Freddy. "Way more."

I didn't see Tara again until third period. Turned out we had English together.

"You again?" I said, slipping into the empty seat next to her.

"Are you following me?" she asked with a smile.

"Yeah, right," I answered. "I spent the morning in the office, rearranging my schedule just so I could have the same third-period class as you."

"I suspected as much," Tara answered, so seriously it took me a second to realize she was matching my sarcasm with her own.

I was surprised to see she was still wearing her mirrored sunglasses in class, and that the teacher, Mrs. Burton, didn't make her take them off.

"Hey, you can't wear those in here," I said, reaching toward the glasses.

Tara smiled and leaned back, easily avoiding my hand. "I have a congenital eye condition," she said. "I need low light all the time, so I have to keep these on. Do you want to see the note from my doctor?"

She put her hand lightly on my shoulder. I was surprised by

how cool it felt, almost cold, even through the material of my shirt.

"Thanks for trying to help me this morning," she said softly. "I didn't mean to be rude or anything."

"That's okay," I said.

The bell rang and class began. Turned out Tara knew a lot about English literature—a lot more than any of the rest of us, maybe even more than Mrs. Burton.

"I think you have to go back to Sophocles," said Tara, "if you really want to grasp the basis of Shakespearean tragedy."

Mrs. Burton looked a little flustered. I wondered if she had any more of a clue about who Sophocles was than the rest of us.

"Well, certainly . . ." she agreed uncertainly.

"And of course," Tara continued, "let's not forget Aristotle's *Poetics,* the foundation of all drama. You can trace a straight line from his theories through Shakespeare to Shaw and all the way to Stoppard. Wouldn't you agree?"

Mrs. Burton was opening and closing her mouth like a fish, but no sound was coming out. Finally, she glanced at the clock. "Well, that's about all the time we have for literary theory," she said, sounding relieved. "Let me give you your homework for tomorrow."

Then the weirdest thing happened.

As Mrs. Burton turned to the board to write down our homework assignment, and everyone started copying it down, I glanced over at Tara. She was looking into the purse of the girl in front of her, Julie Robinson. The open purse was hanging over the back of Julie's chair, and something inside it caught Tara's eye.

Then Tara reached into Julie's purse and took out an antique mirror. It was the one Julie spent half the day admiring herself in—it was her most treasured possession. Tara smiled into the mirror. It was a dazzling smile. She was fluffing her blond curls as the bell rang. Still holding on to the mirror, Tara quickly jotted down the homework assignment that was on the board.

"Tara?" It was Mrs. Burton, approaching. "I want to thank you for elevating the level of discussion in the classroom," she said. "It looks like I'm going to have to do *my* homework, too."

"Thank you, Mrs. Burton," Tara answered smoothly, and Mrs. Burton retreated quickly to her desk.

Tara noticed she still had Julie's mirror in her hand. I watched as she casually slipped it into Kyle Firestone's jacket pocket, without even looking to see where Julie was. Then she glanced at me and smiled—not mischievously, or anything, but like it was nothing. Like taking something from one person and giving it to another was a perfectly normal, natural thing to do.

I didn't tell anyone, and it became the first in a long list of secrets between Tara and me.

5

SOMETHING TERRIBLE, SOMETHING WONDERFUL

When you drop a pebble into a pond, ripples spread out, changing all the water in the pool. The ripples hit the shore and rebound, bumping into one another, breaking each other apart. In some small way, the pond is never the same again.

Tara wasn't a pebble. She was a twelve-ton boulder.

The impact of her presence on our school was felt that very first day, starting with Julie Robinson's freaking out in the cafeteria when she discovered her precious little mirror was gone. She practically foamed at the mouth.

Oh, it was entertaining and all, but things became serious when the mirror turned up in Kyle's pocket. Even though Kyle was a total straight-arrow honor student, no one believed him when he claimed to have no idea how it got there. He was immediately sent to the principal's office.

I said nothing.

When I got home that day, I found myself spending most of the afternoon trying to come up with a good reason to go over to Tara's. I couldn't just show up uninvited like she did. That was her way, but it wasn't mine. I thought that maybe I could tell her I had forgotten a homework assignment—but it was a flimsy excuse, because I could call just about anyone. No, I couldn't make it so obvious. In the end, it was my mother who served as my accomplice, without ever knowing.

"You know, Mom, it's really rude of you not to introduce yourself to the new neighbors," I told her as she sat in the dining room, cutting out pictures of us kids for another one of her scrapbooks.

"Most people like their privacy. They'll introduce themselves when they're ready."

"Tara already did."

Mom gave me a wry look, like she was sucking some meat from between her molars. "Yes—*that* was some introduction, wasn't it."

"I think you should make them one of your famous fruit baskets. Everybody loves those."

Mom considered it. Her fruit baskets truly were famous in our neighborhood, and she prided herself on them. I knew she would want nothing more than to impress the new neighbors with one.

"Check to see if there are any baskets in the basement," Mom said, but I didn't have to check, because I already knew that there were—just as I knew we had plenty of fruit.

It took her almost an hour to craft it to perfection, and of course I dutifully volunteered to take it over.

"You're being awfully helpful today," she said, looking at me suspiciously, as if I had an ulterior motive—which I did.

"He's probably going to eat it on the way," suggested Katrina.

"Don't you dare!" Mom warned.

Five minutes later I was at Tara's door, ringing the bell. I could hear the chimes sound deep within the house, and a moment later, Tara opened the door herself.

"Hey, Baby Baer," she said.

"Hey," I answered back, not bothered by her nickname for me—as long as she didn't use it in front of other people. "Somehow I figured with a mansion like this, you'd have a butler answering the door."

She laughed. "Well, we ran out of food, so we had to eat him."

It was such a weird thing to say I didn't know whether to laugh or what, so I just ended up giggling stupidly.

"But it looks like we won't have that problem anymore," she said, "because now we have fruit!"

"Huh?"

She pointed to the gift basket.

"Oh, yeah, right. Fruit." I held it out to her. "Here's a welcome gift from my mom. She wanted to bring it over herself, but she's under the weather."

"We're all under the weather," Tara said. "If we weren't, we'd be in space, and our lungs would explode."

I was not going to let myself be thrown off balance by her weirdness. "Exactly which mental institution did you escape from?" I asked her. "And is there a reward for your return? Because, hey, I could use some spare cash."

She fluffed her golden curls. "Wanna come in?"

I shrugged like it was nothing. "Sure."

I stepped in to find myself in a grand foyer floored with purple marble and rimmed with white stone statues. She led me into a huge living room with thickly padded furniture—the kind you would sit in and never want to rise out of. I could still smell the aroma of fresh paint. The walls were shocking pink, with moldings and windowsills painted shiny black. It was a weird combination, yet somehow it fit.

"Does color blindness run in your family?"

She put down the fruit basket on a glass table, picking a few grapes for herself. "My family has unique tastes."

"As your butler found out."

She frowned at me then. I didn't expect that. I thought she liked throwing verbal darts at each other. I sure liked it.

"I don't have a butler because my family doesn't believe in hired help," she told me. "We do everything ourselves."

Somehow I had liked it better when she had suggested they had eaten him.

I sat in one of the soft chairs, and it all but swallowed me. "Are your parents around?" I asked. "Should I meet them?"

"They're in Europe with my sisters," she said. "Shopping."

"Couldn't they just go to the mall?"

She didn't answer me, just stared down at me floating in the billows of the chair.

"So then who's here with you? I mean, they didn't leave you alone, right?"

She didn't answer at first, then she said, "They trust me. I'm very self-sufficient."

I have to say it surprised me—our parents got all worried when they had to leave us alone for a single evening. But then I thought, these people are super-rich. Old-money rich. People like that live by their own rules.

"Want the grand tour?" she asked.

"What's it cost?"

She smiled. "A basket of fruit."

"Whew—good thing I had one." I struggled to get out of the deep, comfortable chair.

"This is the living room," she said, and added, "but there's nothing living in here except for me and you."

She led me to a painting on the wall—a Greek temple or something beneath a blazing sky. "As you can see, we pride ourselves on art. Do you like it?"

I shrugged. "It's okay."

"I painted it."

I wasn't expecting to hear that. "You're kidding, right?"

She shook her head. "I've been studying art all my life. This is a view of the Parthenon in Athens. I like to paint pictures of places I've been."

I was still dumbfounded. "So you painted that?"

"Yeah. A few summers ago."

"Wow . . . You're like . . . Mozart, or something!"

"Mozart wrote music."

"I know that—I just mean you're a child prodigy, like him. He wrote symphonies when he was a kid."

She smirked. "So I guess my painting is better than just 'okay.'"

I smiled back.

Tara went on to show me the rest of her house, from the ball-room to the huge pool—but it was the artwork that stuck in my mind. Some paintings were by masters: Monet, Renoir—but even more had been painted by her, and her sisters.

"The three of us are always in competition," she told me. "Actually, I'm glad they're away—it gives me some time to myself."

The more I looked at the paintings, the more impressed I became—but also more troubled. I couldn't say what was bothering me. There was something mildly unsettling about them. Like they were hung just slightly crooked or something. I kept wanting to stare at them to figure out what it was, but she kept me moving through the house.

And then there were the statues. There were dozens of them, and they were amazing.

"Don't tell me you and your sisters did these, too!"

She shook her head. "They came from Europe," she told me. "Most of them, anyway. Some people collect stamps, or coins. My family collects statues."

She claimed that they were just your generic statues, and that none of them were sculpted by the masters, but you could have fooled me. I didn't know much about art. I knew that Rodin was famous for *The Thinker*, and Michelangelo did that famous statue of David—but the marble and granite statues in Tara's house, and around the edge of the pool, were every bit as good as those. The rippling muscles, the expressions on their faces.

When we were done touring the house, she made us banana splits in the kitchen, using fruit from my mom's fruit basket and the richest, most flavorful vanilla ice cream I had ever tasted.

I watched her eat, staring at her like she was one of her own paintings. She caught me watching her, and I began to blush. To hide my embarrassment, I showed her how I could balance a spoon on the tip of my nose like a seal, and she laughed.

"You're funny, Baby Baer."

I tried to think of more ways to make her laugh, until I found myself burping the national anthem—a trick I had learned from Freddy Furbush. I knew I'd feel like an absolute idiot when I got home, but right then, I didn't care.

When I couldn't think of anything else to do, I finished my ice cream, which had long since melted in its little silver bowl. In the silence that followed I thought of something. Something that I had wanted to ask her but hadn't had the nerve to before, because I was afraid it might make her mad. But once you've burped the national anthem, you have the right to ask just about anything.

"Hey, Tara . . . remember that mirror you took from Julie Robinson?"

"What about it?"

"Well . . . why did you do it?"

She shrugged. "It was pretty. I wanted to hold it."

"But you could have asked. . . ."

"Hey, I gave it back, didn't I?"

"No—you put it in Kyle Firestone's jacket pocket."

"Did I? I hadn't noticed."

I knew she was telling the truth; it really made *no* difference to her where she had gotten it or where she had left it.

"It belonged to Julie, not Kyle. How could you not notice that?"

She looked at me for a few seconds, like she was studying me.

"I'll tell you a secret," she said. "Nothing 'belongs' to anyone."

"I've got news for you," I told her. "Communism went out with the Soviet Union."

She rolled her eyes. "It's not about communism; it's just reality."

"I don't know what reality's like where you come from, but in this country, you can't just walk into people's houses whenever you like. You can't take people's things without asking permission. *That's* reality."

She crossed her arms. "Okay—so you're telling me that the shirt you're wearing *belongs* to you?"

I looked down at it. Just a blue T-shirt. "Yes," I said. "It's mine."

I saw an eyebrow rise over the rim of her shades. "You have it now—but someday it'll tear, or you'll outgrow it. Then it will either go to someone else or end up in the dump, buried beneath a ton of dirt."

"Maybe not," I said. "Maybe I'll keep it my whole life."

"And then what?"

"And then what, *what?*"

"And then you die, and even if you take that shirt with you, it *still* ends up buried beneath a ton of dirt."

Suddenly I didn't like the fact that I couldn't see her eyes. "I don't think I like this conversation."

"All I'm saying is that, unless you're immortal, nothing can really belong to you. The best you can hope for is to hold something for a while, but in the end you've got to give it back."

"I don't see what that has to do with Julie Robinson's mirror."

She waved her ice-cream spoon at me to make her point. "Haven't you heard a word I've said? It's not Julie's mirror. The idea of personal property is a myth!"

"Yeah?" I said, getting mad. "Well, sometimes myths are important. Sometimes myths are real."

That gave her pause for thought. She put her ice-cream spoon down gently on the table.

"So they are, Baby Baer," she said. "So they are."

And then she said something that I won't forget until there's nothing left of me but a pile of dust.

"Did you ever have a premonition? A feeling that something terrible was going to happen?"

"S-sometimes," I said. Actually, I always get the feeling that something terrible is going to happen, but usually it doesn't.

Then she leaned in close to me. "I've got a secret for you," she whispered with an unpleasant grin on her face. "Something terrible *is* going to happen. Something terrible . . . and something wonderful."

6

▲

INTERESTING TIMES

I left Tara's place that day feeling weird and a little bit light-headed from being with her. She had that effect on you. Nothing terrible or wonderful happened over the next couple of days, so I figured Tara had just said it to be mysterious and interesting—although she didn't need to say anything to seem mysterious and interesting to me.

During lunch on Wednesday, Tara sat by herself at a table across the cafeteria. Her eyes roved over the other kids eating lunch, and occasionally she stopped to stare through her sunglasses at a select few. I could tell that whoever she stared at suddenly got that creepy sensation they were being watched, then they'd look around to see who it was. When they realized it was Tara, they either got completely self-conscious, or they tried to act cool. But as soon as they responded in any way, Tara lost interest in them and zeroed in on her next target.

I couldn't see her eyes behind her shades, but I got the feeling that she was doing some kind of mental calculation about the people she was studying. She was making connections, putting together the pieces.

Finally, she looked in the direction of Ernest, the captain of the football team. He sat with Melanie at the center table. Ernest and Melanie always sat together there, as if to advertise the fact that they were a couple.

This time Tara didn't turn away when Ernest noticed her. I watched Ernest's expression change. First he seemed nervous and unsure, then he looked flattered, then he boldly returned the look, with just the hint of a cocky smile on his face. It was clear that he had completely forgotten about Melanie's existence for those moments.

This fact wasn't lost on Melanie, who tracked Ernest's gaze to Tara. Nothing was said, but I could tell in that single instant Melanie had lost her boyfriend.

I also knew—or at least I *hoped*—that Tara was just playing. I hoped she had no intention of *really* going out with Ernest. She just didn't strike me as a football jock's girlfriend.

The bell rang. Tara stood up and picked up her tray as she left the table. Most of the kids in the cafeteria didn't know that anything had just happened, but Melanie looked like her universe had just imploded.

The following morning, before class started, I saw Tara talking to Celeste Kroeger.

Celeste was a member of the popular clique of squealing girls that everyone else referred to as the Banshees. The Banshees were as phony as they come. As for Celeste, she was one of the group's underlings and so tried even harder to be phony, with hopes of rising in the ranks.

I had no idea what Tara wanted from her. I mean, sure, the Banshees were the most powerful force in school. They set the social agenda, picked who was "in" and who was "out." They were constant boosters of school spirit and constantly mocked their enemies. Why would any of that possibly matter to Tara? Compared to how exciting Tara was, Celeste and the rest of her group might as well have been made out of Styrofoam.

I walked past the two of them. "Hi, Tara. Hi, Celeste," I said.

Celeste gave me an obligatory nod. The weird thing is that Tara did exactly the same. I kept on walking, but I heard a snatch of their conversation.

"I don't know why you let her tell you what to do," Tara was telling Celeste. "It seems to me that you're a lot smarter than she is."

"Did you know," Celeste said, clearly flattered, "she nearly flunked math last year—she almost had to repeat it."

"I'm not surprised."

I knew they were talking about Melanie, who was Queen Screecher of the Banshees. Melanie gave the orders, and the others followed.

I was hoping to get a chance to talk to Tara at lunch and find out what she wanted from Celeste. I didn't see her in the cafeteria, so I went to the outside lunch tables.

Tara was sitting at a table with Nils Lundgren, the smartest non-geek in the school, a tall, skinny guy with long red hair.

They said he was taking college-level courses in physics and chemistry, but he had a life beyond cracking the books. Even though he bragged that he was one of the only people in the school who knew who to use a slide rule, whatever that is, he could also carry on a normal conversation.

All the true geeks that Nils usually ate lunch with were mumbling to one another a table away, watching with envy as he talked to Tara.

I kept my distance, folded my arms, and watched.

Nils seemed to have lost some of his usual cool around Tara. Like a bad magician doing a stale trick, he kept pulling food out of his bag and offering it to her. First he offered her half of a sandwich, then the other half, then an apple, then a bag of chips, then the apple again. Tara was laughing. Then she asked him something I couldn't hear, and Nils blushed and nodded.

Tara brought out one of her textbooks and opened it on the table in front of them. He looked over the page and then started explaining it to her.

Tara didn't seem like the kind of person who would need anything in a textbook explained to her. I had to find out what was going on.

"Hi, guys," I said, waving to them as I walked up. "What's up?" I tried to sound like I didn't really care as I sat down across from them.

"I'm helping Tara catch up to the rest of us in math." Nils looked at Tara for approval and encouragement. "Her other school used a different textbook, and their curriculum left her about a month behind."

I didn't buy it. Besides, if she was really having trouble in math, she could have asked me. "Do you even remember how to do basic algebra?" I asked Nils. "Isn't that a little beneath you?"

"Algebra is the foundation of all higher math," he said, missing my sarcasm. "It's not something you forget."

"You can stay, Parker," Tara said, "if you really want to."

"I'm sure you'll do fine without me," I answered, walking away from them. "Have fun."

Was it jealousy I was feeling? If so, I didn't know why. Tara wasn't my girlfriend or anything. Not even close. She was just a friend, and barely that.

After lunch, Tara and I both had world history with Mr. Usher. Unlike our English class, though, Mr. Usher believed in assigned seats. I was across the room from Tara, so I couldn't talk to her. As it happened, Ernest Benson was also in Mr. Usher's class, and his seat was next to hers. It seemed to me they were way too friendly.

We were endlessly studying the ancient world, and now Mr. Usher was on ancient beliefs in folklore and superstition. "When things went wrong," Mr. Usher said, "people blamed it on the gods, or fairy folk, or even on their neighbors' placing curses on them."

A few kids laughed, probably thinking, *Those dumb ancient people.*

"One of the simplest Greek curses," Mr. Usher said, "is only one word, accompanied by this gesture." He held up his hand, palm out, then said, *"Na!"*

Some of the kids twittered.

"*Na!* means *there!*" he explained. "That's all there is to it, but according to Greek folklore, it's very powerful and effective."

I thought it was pretty lame myself, but my mind wasn't fully engaged in the subject. Now Tara was slouching back in her seat, exactly the way Ernest was, as if they were soul mates. Ernest was very aware of what she was doing.

I forced my attention back to Mr. Usher.

"Now, one of my personal favorite curses," he said, "is the ancient Chinese curse, *May you live in interesting times.* Does anyone want to take a shot at explaining why that might be a curse?"

I raised my hand. I had no idea what I was going to say, but I had to vent some energy or I would scream.

"Parker?" Mr. Usher said, calling on me, sounding more than a little surprised at my sudden class participation.

"I think it's a pretty good curse," I began unsurely. "*Interesting* is a very, um, interesting word. *Interesting times* can set you up for anything—from something like a plague or an earthquake to smaller problems, like any kind of . . . personal disappointment."

Mr. Usher nodded. "Very good."

I finally had Tara's attention. She glanced over at me with a different expression on her face—one I hadn't seen there before. Could it be that I had impressed her?

The next week flew past. Tara spent more time with Celeste and Nils. She was still working on Ernest, too, although as far as I knew they hadn't exchanged two words. Tara wasn't exactly ignoring me, but she wasn't exactly going out of her way to spend time with me, either. I thought about going over to her house, but that might make me look too needy or pathetic or something. If she wasn't going to make any effort to see me, I wasn't going out of my way to see her.

It was none of my business what she did, I told myself. And anyway, I got the distinct feeling that Tara really didn't care one bit about Celeste or Nils or even Ernest. It seemed to me that she had some other goal in mind, and that she was taking the necessary steps to achieve it.

Something terrible is going to happen, she had said. Was she actually planning something terrible? And if so, why had she let me know? *Because something wonderful was going to happen, too.* Something wonderful to who? To her? To me?

On Thursday, during snack, I sat by myself in the courtyard, digging through my backpack for a packet of mini-doughnuts, when I felt someone sit down next to me. I figured it was one of my buddies, maybe Freddie or Danté, but it wasn't. It was Tara.

"You haven't spoken to me for days," she said. "What's wrong?"

"It seemed like you've been pretty busy getting your social life in order," I said. "I didn't want to get in your way."

She laughed lightly. "You're never in my way, Baby Baer," she said. With hardly any effort at all, she was making me feel like I was special.

Just like all the other people she toyed with.

I pulled away, not willing—not *wanting*—to be one among the others. "You can play that game with Nils and Celeste," I told her, "but it won't work on me."

That only made her smile even broader. "I know," she said, "and I'm glad. No games between you and me. Okay?"

"Okay."

I was trying to think of something else to say, something intelligent, but I didn't get the chance, because right then Melanie stormed up to Tara. She was in tears.

"I hope you're proud of yourself," Melanie said. "Ernest is breaking up with me, thanks to you!"

Tara looked up at her with a half smile on her face. It was an expression that some might have called triumphant. "Ernest?" she said. "I've barely even spoken to Ernest."

I didn't want to be in the middle of this uncomfortable scene, so I stood up and brushed the grass off my pants. "I better get going." I walked about halfway across the quad, then turned around to watch the fireworks from a safe distance.

"You can't fool me," said Melanie. "I've been watching you. I see what you do."

"What do I do?" asked Tara, with only the slightest mocking tone.

"You—you—" Melanie searched for the words. "You *look* at people," said Melanie, only realizing as she said it how stupid it sounded. "You look at people and they . . . change. . . ."

"Oh please," Tara scoffed.

"It's the *way* you look at them," said Melanie, "from behind those stupid shades."

She reached to rip them off Tara's face, but Tara's hand snapped up so fast, you never even saw it move. She smacked away Melanie's hand before it touched her glasses.

"You *don't* want to take these off," Tara said in a very threatening tone. "Trust me. You don't."

"You're a monster," Melanie shouted, still holding her ground. "A monster!"

"Hey!" someone else said. I looked over. It was Nils, followed by the entire Geek Brigade. "Leave her alone."

At the same time, from the other side, Celeste and the Banshees were also closing in.

"Melanie," Celeste said sharply, "this is *so* uncool. We have to talk." Celeste used a different tone with Melanie than usual. I could tell she was no longer taking orders from Melanie.

Across the quad, Ernest stood with some of his buddies from the football team. They strolled over to see what was happening. I noticed that all of his teammates were scowling or snickering at Melanie.

Melanie turned and looked around. The entire school had rallied. The Banshees, the jocks—even the nerds—whole groups that normally weren't even on the same plane of existence had taken sides against her.

Melanie crumbled. She tried to escape the quad, an expression of utter defeat on her face.

Suddenly, Tara's accomplishment was clear. She had lined up allies among the school's various groups and got them all to work together for probably the first time in the school's history. She was like a master builder who could bend materials like stone and steel and clay to her will . . . except her materials were flesh and spirit.

Before Melanie passed me, she stopped and looked at me,

her eyes red and puffy. "Watch yourself, Parker," she told me. "You're in way over your head."

Then she turned away and kept going.

I looked over at Tara, surrounded by her new allies from all the different camps, and she threw me a little sideways wink, making me realize we were in for some "interesting times."

Something terrible is going to happen, she had said. . . .

If it was a time bomb, then what she had done that day had started the clock.

7

DANTÉ'S SECRET

ome on," Tara said. "Now it's your turn to show *me* around."
It was a Saturday afternoon, and we were at my house. This time she had been invited. Mom even prepared her favorite linguini recipe, making it clear that Tara was forgiven for her earlier trespass.

"Show you around? Okay," I said. "This is the living room—"

Tara punched me on the shoulder. "Don't be a jerk," she said, smiling. "I want to see the town. The only places I've been since I moved here are my house, your house, and the school. I want to get an idea of what the whole valley looks like."

"Sure," I said, rapidly thinking about the few points of interest nearby. "What do you want to see?"

"Anything. Everything."

We walked outside. The sun was high in the sky. We had plenty of time to do some sightseeing. I got on my motorbike and looked at Tara.

"Do you have a bike?" I asked.

"Nope," she said. "Slide forward."

I stopped for a second, to make sure I had heard her right. Sharing a seat on a bike was a very intimate thing, usually reserved for a boyfriend/girlfriend level of relationship, and yet Tara was treating it like it was nothing.

"Just a sec," I said, and hurried into the garage to get her a helmet, because how embarrassing would it be if we got pulled over by a cop on our first ride together? Besides, running into the garage gave me time to get that blush off my face, although I don't think I did. I returned with the helmet, hopped on the bike, and she sat down behind me. I kick-started the motor. "Hold on tight." She put her arms around me like it was no big deal, although it felt big dealish to me.

I took off down the long driveway, hanging a left when we hit the street, and soared down the road.

I detoured past friends' homes without her knowing, because I secretly wanted to be seen with her—but of course no one seemed to be around. Then I took her to the most impressive place I knew.

On a nearby ridge, there's a place people called Darwin's Curve, because this was the spot where survival of the fittest really kicked in. In other words, this was where the *really* bad drivers removed themselves from the gene pool by crashing through the railing and plunging a hundred feet to certain death. Even now, there was a gap in the railing from the last accident that had taken place there.

"Here you go," I said, stopping at Darwin's Curve. "You said anything and everything, so here's everything. The whole valley."

I parked the bike at the side of the road. We dismounted and stepped through the gap onto the ridge, a rocky surface that sloped gently for about twenty feet, then plunged down sharply.

Most of the locals—at least those of us without a fear of heights—had no problem walking out to the very edge of the cliff for a breathtaking view. I was carefully making my way toward the edge when Tara fearlessly strode on past me.

"Come on," she said, "if you're not chicken."

"Me? Chicken?" I said, following her. "I live for adventure."

She laughed, almost skipping as she approached the point where the gentle slope turned into a cliff. The little geckos that populated the hills skittered away before her. She stopped at the edge and looked at the town below. The warm wind whipped the twirls of hair around her shoulders.

"There it is," I said, catching up to her. "You can see most of the town from here." I pointed out our school, then Main Street, then the mall. Tara took it all in hungrily.

"Look at all the little, tiny people," she said.

I followed her gaze. I couldn't see any people—just the artifacts of people: buildings, roads, cars.

"They're like toys, aren't they? Little toys we could pick up and play with."

"You're too weird, Tara."

"It's beautiful," she said. "It reminds me of a little town where I once lived, on Crete."

I looked at her. I couldn't tell if she was kidding or not. Crete is somewhere in the Mediterranean Sea. An island south of Greece. As I recalled from Mr. Usher's endless rants on world history, the Minoans lived there until a massive tidal wave wiped them all out. That was one of his more interesting rants.

"You've really been around, haven't you?"

"Oh, yes, I've been around." She nodded, suddenly seeming very far away. "I've been around, and around, and around." Then she smiled. "I have something for you." She checked her pockets and frowned. "Hmm, I must have dropped it. Wait here!" She ran off toward the broken guardrail, disappeared behind a hedge, then returned a few seconds later with something in her hand.

"I think you'll like this."

She handed me a small lizard carved out of stone. It was a gecko, like the ones always running around this place. "This is cool! Where'd you get this?"

She shrugged. "I collect stuff like that. You can have it."

"Thanks!" I carefully slipped it into my pocket. "Come on," I said. "Let's go take a closer look at the town."

We rode down the hill, past the places we had seen from the ridge. I worried that Tara wouldn't find the town quite so attractive up close. The old shopping center, which looked so friendly and inviting from up high, was tired and faded, with its paint peeling and the litter left to fend for itself. The new shopping mall was a prefab monstrosity.

But then there was Main Street, with its antique shops and the old video arcade with cool retro games dating all the way back to the 1980s. It was the only place in town with some character.

The sun was just starting to set as we coasted down Main Street, and we found ourselves caught in that magical moment when the old-fashioned streetlights started blinking on.

I guided my bike to the curb, hit the brakes with a satisfying squeal, and turned off the engine. We were in front of the place where my friends and I hung out—a bowling-alley/coffee shop called Grubbs. Apparently, there used to be an actual bowling alley attached, but it had been torn down. Now all that was left was grubby Grubbs, decorated with bowling-alley furniture and bowling pins on every table. It was kind of pathetic when you thought about it, but the manager was cool and didn't mind if we sat there all afternoon without ordering anything.

"C'mon," I said to Tara. "I'll buy you a soda."

As we went in, I saw Danté and Freddy at our usual booth. Their jaws dropped open when I entered with Tara.

Well, impressing my friends from a distance was fine, but did I actually want to sit at a table with them, where they could find a million ways to embarrass me? No. I started guiding her to the booth farthest away from them.

"Don't you want to sit with your friends?" she asked.

"Not especially."

"Come on," she said. "It'll be fun. You'll see."

We walked up to the booth. "Hey," I said to the two of them, suddenly halfhearted.

"Hey," Danté and Freddy responded. These were my best

friends, but compared to Tara . . . well . . . they kind of seemed like losers.

"Can we join you?" Tara asked.

"Sure," said Danté, sliding over on the padded bench and almost knocking over Freddy's shake in his eagerness. "Come on, sit down, plenty of room."

As if to reward him for his awkwardness, Tara sat down next to Danté, and I sat across from her.

"So you're Tara," Danté said.

"And you must be Danté," said Tara.

"Oh?" he said, brightening. "Heard a lot about me, did you?"

"No," said Tara. "Not really."

Freddy stifled a laugh.

"What's so funny, Freddy?" Tara asked, smiling as she looked at him. "Do you imagine I've heard a lot about *you?*"

I had to admire Tara's light touch. Coming from someone else, these words might have been a real put-down—but coming from Tara, well, Danté and Freddy were acting like it was reward enough just to be the center of her attention. I wondered how she knew their names, though. It wasn't like they were wearing name tags or anything. Did she pick that up at school? Had *I* told her?

"What would you like, Tara?" I asked.

"A strawberry sundae," she answered. "Strawberry ice cream, strawberry topping."

"All strawberries, all the time." I nodded. "You got it."

I walked over to the counter and gave the guy Tara's order, and ordered a root-beer float for myself, keeping an eye on the booth. The conversation obviously wasn't lagging just because I was gone—I saw my friends crack up at something Tara said. I walked back to the booth with my drink and her sundae, setting them down on the table.

Tara grabbed my drink and took a sip. "Mmm," she said, holding on to it. "I like it."

"Um, can I have it back?"

"Nope," said Tara, taking another sip. "You can have my sundae." She pushed it over to me: two pink mounds with lumpy red liquid dripping down the sides. It looked like a piglet that had been squashed by a truck. Roadkill delight.

Normally, something like that would have driven me batty. But there was something about Tara's attitude that made it seem like normal behavior. According to Tara, nothing belonged to anyone, so trying to argue that it was my drink would have been pointless. I ate her sundae, even though I hate strawberries.

"So what do you think of our town?" Danté asked.

"It has a lot to offer someone like me," Tara said. "I think I'm going to like it here."

It's funny, but I felt a wave of relief wash over me. The knowledge that Tara was going to stay awhile calmed a fear that had been growing inside of me—the fear that she was going to leave before I got the chance to know her better. A fear that if our dull town didn't live up to her exotic expectations, she'd be gone. I knew this was completely irrational. I mean, her parents would have some say in the matter, right? Of course I hadn't met her parents yet. They were still somewhere in Europe with her sisters. Shopping. I wondered if anyone else knew that Tara was here all alone. I wondered if I should tell anyone, but knew I wouldn't.

Tara stayed quiet while the three of us talked. Our usual stuff. Danté gave us his predictions on every upcoming sporting event for the next month, while Freddy told us which movies opening over the weekend would be worth seeing and which would be a waste of time.

Tara listened closely, but said nothing. Somehow, though, I got the sense that she was putting my friends under some kind of mental microscope. I could tell she was gathering a lot more information from each of them than just their words—a lot more information than they knew they were giving.

Danté made a point of looking straight at Tara while he spoke, although it didn't really matter, because he couldn't see through her sunglasses. Freddy, on the other hand, had this habit of not looking directly at whoever he was talking to. I noticed that he was sneaking glances at Tara when someone else was speaking, but whenever he was the one talking, he wouldn't look at her.

Freddy was telling us all about some new sci-fi movie while studying his straw, apparently very curious about the technology that made the bendy part possible, when Tara suddenly leaned toward him.

"What's the matter, Freddy?" she asked. "Why can't you look at me? Something on my face you don't want to see?"

Freddy looked startled. "Huh?" He blinked, finally forced to look at her. "What do you mean?"

"When you're talking to someone, it's polite to look at them once in a while." She turned to us. "Doesn't it bother you that Freddy never looks at you when he talks?"

Danté and I exchanged glances. I had never really thought about whether it bothered me, and of course neither one of us had ever mentioned it to Freddy.

"It's not a problem," Tara continued. "It's just a sign of low self-esteem. Does your mother ignore you? Your father belittle you? Something like that?" Tara sighed when Freddy didn't answer. "That's okay. There are worse things in life . . ." And then she shifted her attention. ". . . Aren't there, Danté?"

Danté looked up at her like a rabbit who had just noticed the coyote in front of him.

"Huh?"

"I'm talking about *your* problem."

Danté looked confused for a second, then understanding seemed to dawn on him.

Tara continued. "Your friends don't know about it, do they? But it's on your mind a lot. I know you're embarrassed about it, but you'll feel better if you just say it."

Danté looked at Tara with an expression of disbelief, and Tara returned the look with an expression of infinite sympathy.

"How—how do you know?" he sputtered.

"It's hard to talk about, but you'll feel better if you do. I promise."

Danté looked a little like he was choking on a chicken bone.

Tara continued her soft coaxing. "You want to tell them. I know you do."

"I . . ." Danté began, then stopped.

Tara nodded at him encouragingly.

"I'm afraid of the dark," he said. "Terrified of it. That's why I won't have sleepovers. That's why I don't go to movies." His face was red. His eyes were heavy with tears not quite ready to fall. "One time my night-light went out, and I couldn't stop screaming. So now I have three."

Tara sighed sympathetically. "I understand," she said.

Freddy and I looked at Danté. We were blown away. Cool, confident Danté. The guy with an answer for everything. He suddenly looked so broken, sitting there in the booth. Like Melanie had looked when she had been crushed by Tara.

"Gee, Danté," I began weakly. I don't think I had ever said *gee* in my entire life.

"Y-you never told us," stuttered Freddy.

"It's called nyctophobia," Danté said. "I don't know why I have it, but I do."

It's not like it was such a horrible thing—but that didn't matter, because I guess it was devastating to Danté. He couldn't look at us. I thought for sure he was going to get up and run out of the coffee shop, but he didn't. Instead, he started crying. It was, at the same time, touching and creepy.

I knew I had to say something. "Hey, Danté," I said. "Don't worry about it."

Danté didn't seem to hear.

Then Tara reached across the table and took his hand. With utter conviction and a measure of tenderness, she said, "Listen to me, Danté. It's nothing to be ashamed of, really."

"I sleep with a night-light," I found myself saying.

Danté looked at me and seemed hopeful. "Really?"

It was a lie, but I had to say something. I nodded and smiled encouragingly, but as I did, I was thinking, *I've known Freddy and Danté for almost my entire life and we've never revealed half as much stuff about ourselves in all that time.* Tara had known my friends for less than five minutes, and already she'd ripped them open, pulled their guts out, and then put them back together, slightly different from the way they were before.

It felt like we'd survived a shipwreck together, or maybe a natural disaster. Hurricane Tara.

A dozen thoughts were swimming through my brain, colliding with one another, making it difficult to think straight. I saw my friends in a new light, but I wasn't entirely sure any of us were ready for that—and I had the feeling our friendship had just evolved into a new form. But was it a form that would float, or would it sink like a stone?

A stone . . .

I reached into my pocket and began to fiddle with the lizard Tara had given me, feeling its well-carved scales, the point of its tail, the bulge of its eyes. As I looked at my friends now, in some strange way they seemed not all that different from that lizard. Their expressions were growing harder—a sort of wall suddenly coming down around them, shielding their sudden vulnerability. Like they were turning to stone.

I turned to Tara. She appeared happy and carefree, her golden curls flowing from her head like snakes, almost squirming with each toss of her head.

I rode home with Tara in the dark, the single headlight from my bike lighting the way. As we reached the gate of her mansion, I asked her how she had known about Danté's secret.

"I didn't know *what* it was," she said. "I could just tell that he had a secret. He's the one who gave it away."

"But why did you make him do it?"

I thought she became a little uncomfortable then. Maybe a little serious. "It's what I do," she said. "It's what I am."

"It's how you get your kicks?"

She shook her head. "It's not that simple." Then she sighed. "Listen, it's no big deal. I just took a tiny little nip out of your friends today. Not enough to hurt them . . . just a tiny taste." It was perhaps the weirdest thing in a long line of weird things she had said to me.

"Great," I said uncomfortably. "I'm glad you didn't just swallow them whole."

She looked at me for a long time before she spoke again. A faint crescent moon came out from behind the clouds. I could see it reflected off those glasses that were so ridiculous at this time of night. "Have you ever heard of the alchemists?" she asked.

I almost laughed. I had no idea where that had come from, or where she was going with it. "Yeah—they were in medieval times, right? They tried to turn lead into gold."

She nodded. "They found out that lead can't change into gold." She was silent for a moment, as if weighing what she was going to tell me. It must have weighed quite a lot, because she said it very slowly. ". . . But some things *do* change. . . ."

"What kinds of things?"

"Living things. People."

I was whispering now. Whispering just like her. "How do they change, Tara?"

But she backed away. "Good night, Parker."

Then she turned and hurried through the gate.

When I got home, the security system was on, and no one could be bothered to disarm it for me, so I went around back. I took a moment before I went in, though, to go to the far side of the pool, where that dumb statue of me stood on its pedestal, lit from two sides. Shimmering reflections from the rippling surface of the pool danced across my bronze face, almost making it look alive.

I reached into my pocket then and pulled out the stone gecko. I set the lizard on the pedestal next to my bronze feet, marveling at how it looked so real that it might skitter away at any moment, if it weren't made of stone.

8

▲

THE OIL FIELD

I think she's a vampire or something."

Katrina said it out of the blue while we were playing pool in our game room. She liked to say things just as I was about to shoot, to throw off my concentration. It worked. The cue ball missed the nine ball I was aiming for and went straight into the corner pocket. Scratch.

"Don't be stupid," I told her. "Tara's just like you or me . . . just a little . . . more so."

Katrina got the cue ball and lined up her shot. "Yeah? Well, how come she wears those sunglasses? How come she's always staring at people like she wants to drink their blood?"

"An eye condition. She even wears them at night, when it's dark. And besides, vampires can't be out in the sun at all, or they burn to a crisp—and they hate garlic."

"What does garlic have to do with it?"

"Didn't she eat Mom's Linguini Garlique when she came

over for dinner last week? That stuff has so much garlic *you* won't even eat it. So maybe *you're* the vampire."

Katrina shot, breaking up a cluster of balls, but none dropped into a pocket. "I didn't say she was a vampire. I said she was a vampire or *something.*"

I moved around the table to find a good shot and sank the seven ball. "You're right about that," I said. "Tara sure is something."

Rumors flew through school all the next week about Tara and Ernest Benson. According to the rumors, they had been spotted having burgers at the Pound-a-Beef and going to the movies together. Rumor was they were an "item." I hate rumors.

Tara said absolutely nothing to me about it. I mean, it's not like we were spending all that much time together. We'd get together a couple of times a week to talk or do homework. I couldn't bring myself to ask her about it, so I decided to ask Ernest instead. It was down to the last few minutes of lunch on Friday. Ernest sat alone at a table. Used to be he was with Melanie, or with his football buddies, but lately he'd been eating alone. Tara had already left the cafeteria. It was now or never, so I crossed the cafeteria and sat down across from him.

"Hey, Ernest, what's up?" I said brightly.

"The sky," he answered, like it was something original. He opened a container of milk. There were already four empty ones on his tray.

"So what's with all the milk?"

"I like milk. Is that a problem?"

There was something troubling about his voice. Something in its tone, like his vocal cords weren't resonating properly. Like he was speaking from farther away than he really was. He sounded cold and distant—and when I caught a glimpse of his eyes, they felt cold and distant, too. His eyes were gray—speckled, granite gray—and his pupils were very small, almost pinpricks.

"How come you're not sitting with your friends?" I asked.

"I don't want 'em," he answered. "I don't need 'em."

This was not the Ernest Benson I knew. He had always been outgoing, the center of attention. He was loud, fairly obnoxious, and always funny . . . but he had changed. Or should I say he was changing. Whatever he was becoming, he was only partway there. It was such a strange thought, I had to shake my head to chase it from my mind. I forced myself to remember why I had sat down with him in the first place.

"So it sounds like you and Tara are a couple," I said.

"Who told you that?"

"No one. I just heard."

He finished his milk and crushed the container in his hand. "Then you got lousy hearing."

"So it's not true?"

Ernest looked at me all stone-faced, trying to make up his mind whether he should say anything to me or not. "We went out once. We had burgers and saw a movie. That's all."

I was relieved to know it had only been a single date.

"So . . . you're not going out with her again?"

"No." He offered no more. But now I was curious. I remembered what she had done to my friends Danté and Freddy, picking them apart and putting them back together with her words.

"Why?" I asked. "What did she say to you?"

"She didn't *say* anything. It was the way she looked at me."

I shrugged. "So? She looks at everyone like that."

But Ernest shook his head. "No . . . not the way she looked at *me*." He glanced down at his tray for a moment, then back up at me. "I don't want to talk about it."

I looked down, too, because I didn't want to meet those cold eyes. Instead, I caught sight of his hand on the table. Just like the tone of his voice and the look of his eyes, there was something strange about his hand. Not just his hand, but his skin in general. The awful, flickering fluorescent lights of the cafeteria did have a tendency to paint everyone in morgue tones; but even so, Ernest's skin didn't look right. Not so much pale as gray. Like dolphin skin. *Maybe he's sick,* I thought. *Maybe it has nothing to do with Tara.* "So all she did was look at you?"

"I said I don't want to talk about it." He shook the boxes of milk on his tray, confirming that they were all empty. "Hey, do me a favor," he said. "See that table behind you?"

The kids had left the table behind us, but they hadn't bothered to take away their lunch trays.

"Check the cartons from those trays—see if there's any milk left in them."

I looked at Ernest, not sure I had heard right. "You want to drink other people's milk dregs? What if they backwashed or something?"

"I don't care," Ernest said. "I don't care about anything anymore."

I found him a half-full box of milk, then left without watching him guzzle it.

As for what happened next, it would be easy to say that my brother brought it on himself. It's not like I intended it . . . but then, I didn't stop it, either. You could say I was an accomplice. A partner in crime.

It started innocently enough. Garrett was just leaving the bathroom, drying his hands with a towel. I was in my room doing homework at my desk. I guess I must have been too easy a target for Garrett to resist. There was a snap and a sudden painful sting on my arm.

"Ooh, that's gotta hurt," Garrett said. He stood there with his towel rolled up into a rat tail. He had snapped it at me like a whip. Usually he never does it right, and it doesn't connect, but this time he got it perfect. There was already a painful welt rising on my forearm.

"Garrett, you're dead!"

He just laughed as I chased him out of the room. I grabbed a towel from the bathroom and took off after him down the stairs. I was a master of rat tails, and Garrett knew it—but it turns out I didn't have to use it. On the way down the stairs he lost his footing and did a classic stair tumble, rolling most of the way down.

"Ha-ha!" I shouted, as he hit bottom. "What a loser." He angrily picked himself up and bounded back up the stairs as if I had pushed him. I took off back to my room.

I knew where this was going. I knew where this always went. This was one of those brotherly fights that just keeps escalating until either someone gets really hurt, or a parent gets involved to break it up.

I tried to slam the door to my room before Garrett could get there, but he was too quick. He shouldered his way in and pushed me onto the bed, pounding my shoulder.

"That's what you get for laughing at me!"

"Loser," I said again.

He pounded me one more time, then got up to leave. As he headed out, I reached down and tugged the throw rug that covered the hardwood floor. He stumbled again. "Look at that! You can't even walk out of a room without falling," I said.

He turned to me. "At least I don't have a crush on a girl who thinks I'm a joke," he said. I knew he was talking about Tara.

"She doesn't think I'm a joke!"

"Shows how blind you are!"

Now I could feel my ears getting hot. I knew my face was turning red. "Yeah, well at least . . . well at least Dad won't have to buy my way into college, like he'll have to do for you."

He opened his mouth to speak, then closed it again. It was true Garrett didn't have college-quality grades. His PSAT scores had been frighteningly low. I had hit a nerve, and it was his turn to go red. He looked over at my trophy shelf right next to him, and with a single swift movement, he knocked all my trophies off the shelf.

"No!"

They clattered to the ground, the marble bases cracking, the little plastic men breaking off at the ankles. That's when Mom came into the room.

"What is going on in here? Garrett, did you do this?"

"He broke them! I can't believe it! He broke them!" I got down on my knees, trying to pick up the pieces. It's amazing how many pieces there were. I could feel tears of fury coming to my eyes now.

Garrett just looked down at me. "What does he need them for?" he said. "He's got a life-size one in the backyard."

I don't know what possessed me to do what I did next, or what I even hoped to accomplish, but I stretched out my hand, palm forward at Garrett and said:

"Na!"

It was that old Greek curse Mr. Usher had told us about, but Garrett didn't know that. He just ignored it, staring me down like a mad dog, then stormed out.

"Garrett!" shouted Mom, but he was gone. I was gone a second later, but I didn't follow Garrett. Our battle had ended. He had won. I bounded down the stairs.

"Parker, where are you going?" Dad asked as I passed his study.

"Out."

"Out where?" He swiveled back and forth in his special desk chair—the one Tara had sat in the first time she trespassed in our house. I was out the front door before he could question me anymore. I never used to be secretive with my parents. I never had anything to be secretive about. But I was changing bit by bit. I was getting a little harder. Harder to read, harder edged.

I went straight to Tara's. I shouldn't have. I should have taken the time to calm down, but when you're mad, you don't see clearly enough to know that you're not seeing things clearly.

When I got there, Tara must have seen in my face how angry I was.

"Having a bad day, Baby Baer?"

"You're lucky your sisters are on the other side of the Atlantic. I wish my brother was, too."

"Sounds like you could use a specialist in sibling removal."

"Not removal, just torture," I said. "I want him to suffer."

She laughed, and instead of inviting me in, she stepped out, closing the door behind her. "You've shown me your favorite place," Tara said. "Now let me take you to mine. Get your dirt bike."

I did as she said. I went back, got my bike out of the garage, and met her at her front gate. "I'll drive this time, you ride in back," she said.

"Where are we going?" I asked.

"You'll see."

I rode on the back of my own bike as Tara went winding through the streets of our expensive neighborhood, then turned down an old dirt path I never even knew existed. All the while, I felt this tingle of excitement. I was free-falling into one of Tara's mysteries, and I liked the feeling.

For miles we wound between huge, old oaks that nearly

blocked out the sun. Then we came out into a remote clearing filled with half a dozen giant praying mantises.

"What the . . . ?" I nearly fell off the back of the bike. The green creatures rose about twelve feet high, their heads as big as my whole body. Tara stopped the bike sharply, kicking up a cloud of dust that filled my nostrils, making me sneeze.

"Do you like it?"

It took a few moments for my mind to process what I was seeing. These weren't giant insects; they were oil wells. Not the kind that tower high, but the kind that pump up and down, looking something like big bugs. But these had been painted green with big bug eyes. None of them were moving. In our town it wasn't unusual to find these old, abandoned oil pumps, but I don't think anyone knew about this forgotten cluster—and I certainly didn't know they were painted green.

"You painted them like this?"

"I thought they were too ugly painted gray."

"When did you find the time to do this?"

Tara shrugged as she got off the bike. "Sometimes I can't sleep."

As I looked around, I laughed. Six big bugs filled the clearing, and no one but Tara and I knew.

"These things are balanced by counterweights," she said. "I've oiled the gears. It doesn't take much to get them moving."

Together we leaned on the great mechanical beasts, bit by bit getting them to pump up and down, until the clearing was full of great green, bobbing bugs. Then we sat down in the middle of it all, the smell of old oil filling the air, and the strained sound of tired gears grinding out the afternoon. I asked Tara why she had bothered to paint them, and again she just shrugged. "Sometimes," she said, "art's only purpose is to make the artist happy." But she had succeeded in more than that, because being in the middle of this strange moving symphony made me happy, too.

"I spoke to Ernest," I finally told her.

She didn't appear troubled at all. "We had a fun evening out. I won't be seeing him again."

"Yeah, that's what Ernest said." Then I took a deep breath and asked her what I was really thinking. "Tara . . . am I . . . am I just a joke to you?"

"Never," she answered, without hesitation. "Why would you think that?"

"Just something my brother said."

"Your brother, Garrett," she repeated. It bothered me that she knew his name. "Is he horrible to you?"

"He's just an idiot."

"You had a fight?"

I shrugged. "It was stupid. He ended up breaking my trophies." I thought for a moment, then added, "So I told him, 'Na!'"

"The Greek curse!" Tara said. "Good for you!"

I laughed, because she didn't. She took it seriously. She took *me* seriously. We didn't say anything for a long time. We just listened to the groaning gears of the bobbing bugs as they pumped empty wells.

"What are you afraid of, Parker? What are you afraid of more than anything else?"

It was a strange question, but not coming from Tara. If she *hadn't* asked a strange question, I would have started to worry. "I don't know. Dying, I guess."

"That's what everyone says, but it's not true. People are more afraid of other things. Think. What do you *really* fear?"

I closed my eyes and thought. I wasn't in the habit of dwelling on what frightened me—I usually had better things to do—and it wasn't very often that I was challenged to think too deeply. I wasn't sure I liked it.

"What am I afraid of?" I said, stalling. "I'm afraid of . . . being forgotten." I wasn't sure I meant it until I said it. I opened my eyes. "I mean, I guess we all have to die someday, but to live and have such a pointless life that you're forgotten right after you die . . . that's what I'm most afraid of."

Tara smiled. "I believe you. I believe you're telling the truth."

I gazed toward the mantis heads again. They were slowing down. They could move only so long from the momentum we had given them.

"What if I told you that you WILL make a difference," Tara said. "What if I told you that you don't even have to die?"

I turned to her. Was she crazy? In the half-light of twilight, with Tara sitting there wearing her mirrored shades, it sure seemed possible. No. More likely she was just trying to freak me out again. She liked doing that. And I liked when she did it. This time, though, it felt one step over the edge.

"If you told me that, I would say you were nuts."

She didn't have any answer to that.

"My sister thinks you're a vampire," I spouted out in the discomfort of the moment.

Tara laughed. "A vampire? Hah! I wish it were that easy. I wish it were that simple." She sighed. "Well, Parker, rest assured that I don't drink blood or turn into a bat."

"My sister will be relieved." I moved a little bit closer to her. "How about you, Tara? What are you afraid of?"

I could see her shoulders move uncomfortably, like she had a chill. "Never mind that."

"C'mon, you asked me. Why can't I ask you?"

She looked at me through those impenetrable lenses of hers. I wondered if this was the way she had looked at Ernest—or if that look had been something different.

"I'm afraid of . . ." She took a long time to think about it. ". . . more of the same."

I didn't know what it meant, but I could tell she was being honest. "So, is sitting here with me more of the same?"

"No," she answered. "Being here with you is . . . new." Then her tone of voice suddenly changed. She became more focused. "I want you to do something for me," she asked.

"What?"

"I want you to introduce me to your brother."

I shifted uncomfortably. "Why would you want me to do that?"

"Maybe I want to get to know him," she said. "Maybe I think he's cute." And then she whispered, "Or maybe I just want to prove to you that you're not a joke."

And although I had no idea how meeting my brother might prove anything to me, I agreed to introduce them. I wanted to say something to her that sent all of her feelings spinning out of whack, like she had just done to me, but I couldn't tweak people like that. Especially not her. Tara was untweakable.

We sat there in silence until the sun was below the horizon and the mantis heads had all ground to a halt. But there was a gear work still moving—a silent machine that was all Tara's—and I knew that whatever she was planning, I was helping to grease the gears.

9

▲

THE FIRST LOCK

Even though I didn't understand her request, I was curious. Tara never did anything without some larger plan. Introducing her to Garrett was not going to be fun. Garrett would do his best to make me look bad in front of her and make himself look good. The only good part about it was that I had complete control over the time and place. I put a little thought into it and came up with a perfectly wicked way to introduce them.

I swung by Tara's place on my dirt bike the next Saturday afternoon to take her to the mall. It was before Halloween, and the mall was a zoo with shoppers, and I knew that Garrett would be hard at work. He had a part-time job at the Pound-a-Beef, everyone's favorite awful fast-food place. He worked there not because he needed the money, but because Mom and Dad insisted he develop some sort of work ethic, just in case he couldn't fake his way through the rest of his life.

This was where I would introduce Tara to him. I wanted Garrett to be in the position of having to serve us. "Hi, Garrett—this is Tara," I would say, and I imagined him going all red in the face when he had to say, "Hi, Tara. You want fries with that?" What a great moment it would be. And besides, he'd looked like a moron in the beige-and-pink uniform he had to wear.

I didn't tell Tara any of this, of course. I wanted her to be as unprepared as Garrett for the meeting. Whatever her game was, she was going to have to think on her toes.

We got to the Pound-a-Beef just after the lunch rush. Garrett was at the second register. He hadn't noticed us yet because he was busy taking an order from a woman with two bratty kids.

"No, no," the mom was saying. "Ketchup."

"So that's two burgers, one with no ketchup?" Garrett said.

"Extra ketchup! *Extra ketchup!*" howled one of the kids.

"Oh," said Garrett, staring cluelessly at the readout on his register. "I thought you said extra mustard."

The woman sighed. "I said no mustard on the first, and extra ketchup on the other, double cheese, but no tomato, put their onions on my burger, and fries. Well-done."

"Fries well-done?" said Garrett, quickly punching buttons on the touch pad in front of him.

"No, the burgers!"

I held back a laugh. He would definitely look like a moron to Tara now. Finally, he completed the order, collected the woman's crumbled bills, and said, "Next, please."

As soon as he saw it was me, he started to scowl. "No free lunch for family members," he said. "You want to eat; you pay like everyone else."

Garrett's eyes shifted to my left. I could see him freeze up slightly when he saw Tara.

"Oh," I said, trying to sound casual and effortless. "Tara, this is my brother, Garrett. Garrett, Tara."

They shook hands. "So you're the infamous Tara," he said, grinning.

"In the flesh."

"Nice shades."

"I got them on the French Riviera."

I rolled my eyes. "Can we order now?"

"Sure," said Garrett. "What do you want?"

Tara and I placed our orders, but as I reached for my wallet, Garrett held up his hand and said, "Well, whaddaya know! I accidentally rang it up for free." And he winked at Tara. I was too stupefied to say anything. "I guess it's on the house," he said.

"That's awfully sweet of you," said Tara, smiling. "By the way, I like that uniform on you. That color combination suits you. Very fashion forward."

Garrett puffed up like a balloon. "Thanks."

Tara smiled at him a bit too long, then he went off to get us our food.

Tara and I sat uncomfortably on the plastic chairs at the plastic table, chewing our plastic food. "What was that all about?" I asked. No sense hiding how annoyed it all made me feel.

"Be a good boy, Baby Baer," she said. "Play your part, and you'll have your reward."

I heard someone approaching and turned to see Garrett. He

pulled up a chair beside us. "Aren't you supposed to be working?" I asked, irritated.

"I'm on my break," he said. "I thought I'd take it with my little brother."

I squirmed in my seat, but said nothing.

"So, Tara," Garrett said, "done any more breaking and entering lately?"

"I think trespassing is the most I could be charged with," Tara answered, smiling. Then she reached for a fry and knocked over her drink. She tried to make it look like an accident, but I knew it was intentional. Orange soda poured onto the floor, splattering my shoes.

"Oops! Parker, could you get me a refill?"

"Have Garrett get it," I said. "He works here."

"But I asked *you*." She held up her empty cup to me. I stared at it for a moment, then grabbed it in frustration and left. Play my part. Play my part. Was this my part? Fetching her a drink? Fetching her my brother? What else was I supposed to fetch her?

I refilled her soda, silently stewing to myself, and by the time I returned I knew that something had changed. Some deal had been struck between the two of them while I was gone.

As soon as I sat down, Garrett got up. "Well, I'd better get back to work," he said. "See you tonight, Tara." Then he left.

I turned to Tara for an explanation. "What about tonight?"

"Garrett's taking me for a ride in his Lexus," she said. "Then we're going to the rodeo—it's in town this weekend."

I was speechless for three seconds that felt like twenty. "*I* was going to ask you to the rodeo!"

But instead of answering, she looked at me thoughtfully. All I could see was my own frustration reflected back at me in her lenses. Then she reached out and caught a lock of my hair just next to my left temple. She wrapped it tightly around her finger.

"What are you doing?"

"You'll see," she said. She took her hand away and smiled, satisfied. I had no idea what that was all about until I went to the bathroom a few minutes later and caught sight of myself in the mirror. There, just in front of my left ear, a clump of my normally straight hair seemed like it had fused together. It now hung in a tightly wound auburn curl.

I left the mall and rode Tara home without saying another word to her. Then I rode my bike up and around the hills outside of town until I didn't know what time it was. Had Tara been using me to get to Garrett, or was she plotting something against him? Was I a conspirator, a stooge, or a victim? The curl she had weirdly, miraculously given me was like a worm squirming its way through my head. I wanted to stop thinking about everything, but I couldn't.

My aimless riding took me past Dante's house, and I saw him and Freddy playing basketball on his driveway. It's funny, but ever since that night with Freddy and Dante in the coffee shop, I hadn't been that interested in hanging out with them—and just because I *didn't* feel like playing ball with them, I forced myself to go over and do just that.

"Hey," I said.

"Hey," Freddy answered. Then he passed me the basketball. It was the usual greeting, but it didn't feel usual anymore.

I dribbled slowly up the court toward the basket. Danté tried to block me, but with a burst of speed I blew past him and hit a perfect layup, feeling the ball roll off my fingertips and into the hoop. I don't think I had ever jumped so high.

"Hey, it's no fun if you're not even gonna try," I said to Danté, mocking his effort.

"Two on one," Danté said to Freddy. Freddy nodded.

"Fine," I said. "You're on."

Freddy and Danté had both been on the team with me last year. In fact, they had stayed on the team after I had lost interest. They were pretty good, but the way I was feeling at the moment—with energy to burn and the need to burn it—they might as well have been playing hopscotch.

I stole the ball from Freddy, leaped up to the basket, and practically dunked it.

"Hey!" Freddy said. "Foul!" But it wasn't a foul, and he knew it—I had stolen the ball with such speed and skill, he hadn't even noticed where the ball had gone until he saw it in my hands.

I soon lost count of the score. It didn't matter. I just knew that no matter how well they were playing, I was hitting three baskets for every one of theirs.

We burned out in less than half an hour, and when we were done, the three of us lay on our backs on the driveway, knees bent to the darkening sky. The cement was still warm long after the sun had hidden itself behind the trees.

"If you keep playing like that," Freddy said to me, "they'll draft you right into college ball. Never mind that you're not on the team anymore."

"Coach woulda flipped to see you play like that," Danté said.

We caught our breaths for a few more moments, then Danté sat up and looked at me. "So what's with the hair?" he asked. "A new look?"

I touched the tightly spun lock dangling just out of my vision. I could feel it tugging on me, as if Tara's finger were still wound up in it, pulling it tight. "I don't know," I said. "Maybe. Ask me again tomorrow."

But I knew they wouldn't ask me tomorrow. Just like I knew I wouldn't be hanging out with them much anymore. It was like I could sense a door closing behind me as a new one opened in front of me. Danté and Freddy . . . well . . . they were just on the wrong side of that closing door.

I went home and just sat in my room in the dark. So a door had closed behind me, but I wasn't sure I liked the one opening in front of me . . . because Tara was out with Garrett. Garrett was gone by the time I got home, and I knew where he was. I could just imagine them sitting together at the rodeo, sharing popcorn and cotton candy. It should have been *my* cotton candy she was sharing. At that moment I hated my brother so much, I could feel it like a fever burning behind my eyes.

I didn't know what time it was when I heard his car pull into the driveway, but it must have been late. I waited for the front door to open. When it didn't, my curiosity got the best of me and I moved to my window and peered out.

I could see Garrett's Lexus in the driveway. No one got out. Our yard lights were bright enough for me to make out a single figure in the car, behind the driver's seat. Garrett was alone, and he was sitting as still as a statue. It wasn't like him; Garrett was usually out of his car before it stopped rolling.

Finally, as though pulling himself from a trance, Garrett opened the car door. The interior light flicked on, and I could see him better as he climbed stiffly out of the car and rose unsteadily to his feet.

I met him at the front door.

"How was the rodeo?" I asked as he walked in the house. I had been practicing my delivery of that line for hours. Bitter. Nasty. An accusation more than a question. My tone of voice was lost on Garrett, however, who seemed a million miles away.

"Huh?" he asked, blinking his eyes several times, as though he couldn't see me in the dim light of the entryway.

"The rodeo? With Tara?"

"Fine. It was fine." He stumbled past me. "Man, I'm thirsty."

I followed him into the kitchen. "How about Tara? Did she think it was 'fine'?"

Garrett poked his head into the refrigerator. In the colorless, cold light, his face looked a sickly shade of pale. He found a can of soda and popped it.

"Are you listening to me? I asked you about Tara."

He took a few swallows from the can, then gagged and spat it out into the sink. "That's rank."

I took the can away from him. "What's wrong with you? Are you deaf? I asked you a question."

He spotted a half-gallon carton of milk in the fridge, grabbed it, and chugged it all the way down. Little rivers of milk spilled from the corners of his mouth. Garrett has always made a habit of ignoring me, so that wasn't all that unusual—but you first have to notice someone before you can ignore them.

I grabbed his arm and forced him to face me. The milk carton dropped to the ground, but he had already emptied it.

"What happened tonight?" I asked, speaking each word slowly and clearly.

Garrett looked at me. It seemed like he was trying to remember who I was. Finally, he shook his head and for a moment seemed to come back from whatever mental vacation he was on.

"To tell you the truth, Parker, I don't remember. Isn't that a hoot?"

And I believed him. It didn't make any sense at all, but I believed him. I turned, troubled, and started to walk away, but then he suddenly spoke up.

"I do remember one thing, though. I do remember one thing."

I turned back to face him. He was staring off into the distance, like an old man trying to remember things that had happened to him a long time ago.

"I do remember one thing," he said again.

"What?" I asked, afraid to hear the answer.

Then he looked straight at me.

"She took off her glasses."

10

Becoming Igor

Lethargy. It's a word I know, because it's in one of my father's favorite expressions. *Lethargy breeds lethargy.* It means the more you lie around doing nothing, the more you *want* to lie around doing nothing. Your limbs and your mind feel so heavy that it becomes a major effort just to lift your arm to channel surf.

When you've got money and time, lethargy becomes like a disease. You've got so many choices of things to do that nothing seems worthwhile anymore. That's the way it had been with me and basketball. That's the way it had been with me and so many other things. I remember how my friends and I used to hang around on weekends, saying to one another, "So what do you want to do?" only to get shrugs and the same question back. After a while on those long, boring weekends, it would feel like your body was turning to stone and your mind was turning to mush. I never really thought about it much, but seeing Garrett acting so strangely started me thinking about a lot of things.

Laziness and attitude ran rampant at my school, so maybe that's why it took so long for people to notice the hardening of the social arteries. It began with Ernest, then spread with the tireless growth of a creeping vine. I knew the symptoms. The dull, pasty skin. The glazing of the eyes, and a weariness that went bone deep. I could spot them in the lunchroom. The girl who would lift her spoon to her mouth as if her arm were moving through dense Jell-O instead of air. There was the guy in English class who, when everyone else rushed out with the bell, would take a deep, shuddering breath and rise from his seat like Atlas with the world on his shoulders. And then there was the thing about food. That was perhaps the strangest of all.

It was on the last day Danté, Freddy, and I hung out together. We sat at lunch, chowing down on what we liked to call Roadkill Roast—an oversalted, semi-edible pot-roast substance that the cafeteria served. It was nice out that day, so most kids sat at the outdoor lunch tables. Then, a few tables over from us, Celeste Kroeger, of Banshee fame, dropped her tray on the ground, flipping her Roadkill Roast into the dirt.

"Best thing that could happen to the stuff," Danté commented. "Now all she has to do is kick some dirt over it and give it a decent burial."

But that's not what she did. Instead, Celeste knelt down and picked up the strips of pot roast one by one . . . and pushed each one into her mouth.

"Oh, gross!" Freddy said. Danté and I were beyond even those words. We just stared. You know the "three-second rule"? That brainless notion that if food hits the ground, it's not dirty if you get it off the ground in three seconds? Well, when something falls into mud, that doesn't really apply. There was more mud on those strips than there was beef.

"I think I'm gonna hurl," said Danté.

"Don't," I told him. "She might eat that, too."

We just watched, stupefied, as Celeste pulled every last piece of pot roast, every carrot fragment, every little shriveled pea out of the mud and ate it, licking her fingers when she was done. Then she washed it down with a container of milk. It made me shiver, because I thought of the way Ernest had guzzled those leftover milks from empty tables. The way my brother downed a half gallon the other night.

"She didn't even wipe the mud off the meat," Danté said.

"She liked it," I told them, and the more I thought about it, the more certain I was that it was true. "She liked the dirt more than the meat."

Danté stuck out his tongue. "Well, that's just sick."

And although I had to agree, it brought to mind something I had heard about cravings. People think pregnant women crave pickles, but the truth is, each pregnant woman craves something different. It has to do with what your body needs at the time. My mom craved lemons every day that she was pregnant with Katrina. I always used to say that's why she turned out so sour. It's not only pregnant women who have cravings, however. Celeste was having a strange craving for some other reason. I *have* heard of people craving mud. That was supposed to mean your body needed certain minerals. But craving and eating are two different things.

"She's gone nuts," Freddy said, and left it at that. They thought this was an isolated incident, just one freakish girl with a weird taste for muddy meat—but I wasn't so sure. Over the next few days, I kept an eye out for things like it, and I found that there was a whole earthen feast going on.

. . . Like the girl in ceramics class who, while throwing a pot on the spinning wheel, didn't just use her fingers; she leaned over and began shaping the pot with her tongue.

. . . Like the girl who dipped her hand into her boyfriend's trail mix, only to find there were actual parts of the *trail* mixed in with the nuts and raisins.

. . . Like the kid who kept biting his fingernails just to get at the black nail jam underneath.

. . . And like Celeste Kroeger, who kept knocking her plate "accidentally" into the mud, day after day, then scooping it back up from the ground and eating it, mud and all.

I asked Tara about it as we sat one afternoon having a picnic among the bobbing insect heads of our secret oil field. She just shrugged.

"People are weird," she said. "Haven't you figured that out yet?"

"Yeah—but eating dirt and rocks and stuff? I mean, what could make a normal person do something like that?"

"The key word here," said Tara, "is *normal*. A normal person wouldn't."

"So then you agree that there's something up with them?"

Again she just shrugged—but a little less comfortably this time. "Could be just some stupid, trendy thing they saw on TV.

I read about some kids who heard you could get drunk on water, so they drank so much that they got brain damage. Stupid."

I ate my sandwich, mercifully free of anything that wasn't supposed to be in there. No sand, no rocks. A side of me wanted to leave the whole situation alone, but there was another, darker side that couldn't let it go. It was the same side of me that somehow sensed Tara knew more than she was telling. Sometimes, though, you make a pact with yourself. *I'll pretend there's nothing wrong if you pretend there's nothing wrong.* It's called denial, and it's one of the strongest pacts in the world. Just ask all those people who were still drinking champagne while the *Titanic* went down.

I was standing on the rocky slope at the edge of the cliff just beyond Darwin's Curve. A gentle breeze blew my hair in and out of my eyes as I looked out over the town below.

I was alone.

No, someone was with me—behind me. I could feel it. I wanted to turn around and see who it was, but I couldn't. I was frozen. All I could do was stare down at the town. It seemed so tiny. So fragile.

Whoever was behind me was closer now, inches from my back, and suddenly I was afraid—afraid that this person would push me over the edge of the cliff. I could sense hands about to touch my back and give me a shove.

I saw a sudden movement on the ground beneath me—a shadow. The shadow of a headful of snakes. No—not snakes. Twirls of curly hair.

It was Tara.

I sighed with relief and felt my body relax. I was safe.

Then I felt her hands connect with my back, hard—and I tumbled off the edge in a mad free fall, until . . .

. . . I woke up in bed.

I had known it was a dream from the very beginning—sometimes you just do . . . but that didn't change how powerful it had felt. Dreams can twist your emotions like no reality can.

I got out of bed and made my way to the bathroom. Dim light streamed in through the window, and I saw myself in the mirror. Something in my hair caught my eye.

My twisted curl.

It seemed to sparkle, catching the early morning light. I flicked on the bathroom light, leaned over the sink, and took a closer look.

My own hair is light brown, but this twirl appeared to be made of many different colors, combining strands of black, red, different shades of brown from dark to light, blond, and even silver.

And then I saw it twitch.

It must have been a trick of the light, or maybe my head had moved. I put my chin in my hand and held my head as still as I could. The hanging curl didn't move. I held my position there to make absolutely sure. A minute. Two minutes. Finally I relaxed and looked away only for an instant.

And the curl twitched again. I caught it only out of the corner of my eye, like the ghosts you see late at night after you've spent too much time watching TV.

I yanked open the drawer and looked for scissors, but I

couldn't find any. I slammed the drawer in frustration, then threw on some clothes and headed downstairs.

The rest of the family was already eating breakfast. Katrina noisily munched her cereal. My parents drank coffee and ate English muffins while sharing the paper. Garrett lifted his cereal bowl to his mouth, guzzling the rest of his milk.

"Gross!" Katrina shouted, pointing at my head. "Parker has a worm in his hair."

"It's not a worm," I said, taking a seat and grabbing the box of cereal. "It's just hair."

"It's like Tara's!" Katrina squealed.

"Yeah, but I'm getting rid of it."

My dad now looked thoughtfully at my brother. "Got enough milk there, Garrett?"

Garrett was pouring more milk into his empty bowl, nearly filling it.

"Huh?" Garrett looked down at his bowl, as though seeing it for the first time. "Oh, right. Cereal."

He snatched the box from me, reached inside, and grabbed a handful of colorful loops. He dropped them into his bowl, and a thin layer of cereal spread out across the deep lake of milk. Garrett picked up his spoon, scooped up the few floating cereal-bergs, then lifted the bowl and sucked down the rest of the milk. He didn't seem to notice that we were all still staring at him, because when he was done, he poured himself yet another bowl of cereal-less milk.

"Garrett," said my dad, touching his arm. "Are you feeling okay?"

Garrett pulled away. He never liked it when anyone touched him.

"I'm getting the thermometer," Mom said.

As soon as she left the room, Garrett stood up.

"I'm outta here," he announced. His exit might have been more dramatic, but instead of storming out in his usual spring-legged stomp, he just kind of shuffled away, like every step was an effort.

"What's wrong with this family?" Katrina asked.

I finished the rest of my cereal. I didn't have an appetite anymore, but at least eating took my mind off Garrett's strange behavior.

I sat outside by myself at lunch. I didn't feel like sharing my space with anyone, but I could hear them talking. About me. I knew they were staring at me and my dangling curl.

I could feel it twitch.

I sat on the edge of the quad, looking at the other kids in groups of twos, threes, and fours. They were laughing, talking, relaxing. They looked so far away to me: distant and remote, as if I would never be part of their world again. I knew if I wanted to I could just walk over to any table and start talking to them, and I'd be accepted—welcomed, even—but I didn't want to. Not then, anyway.

I heard someone behind me, and before I could turn around to see who it was, I heard: "Hi, Baby Baer."

I stiffened, then relaxed again.

Tara sat down. I looked at her for a long time, but as always, I could only see myself reflected in her shades.

"What's wrong?" she asked.

"What happened that night you went out with Garrett?"

"Still worried about your brother?" Tara said with a smile. "You shouldn't be."

I stared at her and said nothing. She sighed.

"Nothing happened," she said. "We went out to the rodeo, then played a few lame carnival games. That's all. We won't be going out again."

"He's acting strange at home."

She shrugged. "Why is that my problem?"

I began to feel a little guilty for accusing her—although I don't even know what I was accusing her of. I nodded and even managed a small smile. "Yeah, you're right," I said.

"Good," she said. "I'm glad that's settled. Now . . . what can you tell me about Leticia Fernandez?" She reached up and turned my head toward another table, where Leticia and a few of her friends were chatting.

"Not a lot." I tried to dredge up all I could remember about her. "She's on the drill team. I think she's an artist or something. I hardly know her. Why?"

"I want you to introduce me to her. I have a feeling the two of us can be good friends."

I tried to make sense of Tara's request and couldn't. I slowly shook my head, confused. "What do you need me for, Tara?" I asked. "You can introduce yourself to her. Everyone here knows who you are."

"I know I could do it myself, but I don't want to. I want *you* to do it."

"Why?"

Tara slid closer to me. I couldn't read the expression on her face.

"You're not like them anymore, are you, Baby Baer?" she said. "Can't you feel it? You're changing. You can act like you still fit in, but you really don't."

Tara reached out and wrapped another strand of my hair around her finger. I should have pushed her hand away, but I liked that feeling of her finger twisting in my hair way too much.

"I feel like you're playing games with me," I said.

She shook her head. "It's not a game, Parker. It's not a game at all. Think of it as a gift: *your* gift, to me. But you'll get something back, too. Something that will make it all worthwhile."

She kept talking as she twisted my hair around her finger. "All you have to do is trust me, Parker. I need you to trust me. You, of all people."

She released my hair. And although I couldn't see it, I knew what she had given me. I knew because I could feel the way it twitched.

"You're growing, Parker," she said.

"Growing?" I asked. "Into what?"

"You'll see."

Like I told Tara, I didn't know Leticia very well, but she knew me. She was one of the cheerleaders who had cheered me on when I was the star of the basketball team last year.

"Hey, Leticia," I said to her later that day. I was sitting on a bench near the entrance to the gym, pretending to study, pretending I wasn't lying in wait. I'd probably never spoken to her the entire time we'd been at school together. If she was surprised that I was talking to her now, she didn't show it.

"Hi, Parker. What's up?"

"The usual. You know. Where are you headed?"

"Um, lunch? The cafeteria?"

"Hey, cool, I'll walk over with you." I felt like an absolute idiot. I didn't know what I was saying, or what I was going to say next, but it was too late to stop. "It's been a while since we talked, huh?"

"I don't think we ever talked. I didn't think you even knew I was alive."

"Sure I knew," I said. "I always saw you, cheering on the sidelines. You were the one who jumped the highest."

Leticia smiled and shook her head. "No," she said, "*you* were the one who jumped the highest. I'm sorry you're not playing anymore."

I don't know why I'd never talked to her before. She seemed nice. And she was pretty, too. How come I'd never really noticed her until now? Until it was too late.

Too late? Why did I think that?

When we entered the cafeteria, I saw Tara not far away, sitting with her back to us, eating by herself at a table. Like we had planned.

For about five minutes my life had seemed normal again, a feeling I hadn't realized I'd been missing.

"Nowhere to sit," Leticia said, scanning the cafeteria.

"Hey," I said casually, "there's Tara. Do you know her?"

"No," Leticia said, "we haven't met. Although I've heard a lot about her."

"Oh yeah?"

"Rumors, mostly—she's filthy rich, and her family dumped her here."

"Actually, she's a friend of mine," I said. "She's not that bad."

"I'm sure she's not," Leticia said quickly. "They were just rumors. I'm really curious about her. It seems to me like she must be very lonely. Why don't we go sit with her?"

"You want to?" I asked.

"Sure."

"Okay. Come on, I'll introduce you."

And that was that. I had led this pretty, unsuspecting fly into the web, and she never even knew. As we walked toward Tara's table, I had a mixture of feelings in the pit of my stomach: so many different feelings that I couldn't pick them apart. The strongest was a feeling of dread, followed by the feeling that I was doing something incredibly wrong. But there was also a feeling of pride, the feeling that I had accomplished what I had set out to do, and a warm glow that came from making Tara happy. I pushed all the feelings, good and bad, farther down into the pit of my stomach, hoping that I could just quietly digest them.

Tara and Leticia hit it off immediately. Soon they were giggling together like they had known each other for years. When lunch was over, they walked off together without a word to me. Tara didn't even glance back.

Of course a few days later, Tara was back at my side. As for Leticia . . . well, I didn't see her in school that day. I didn't make a point of looking for her, either.

"There's someone else I want to meet, Parker."

It was morning, before school started. No one else was around. I was sitting under a tree in the quad. This time I didn't bother looking up.

"Who?" was all I said. "Where and when?"

"I want you to introduce me to Josh Weinstein."

Josh was the best actor in the drama department by far. He had been the lead in every play since he had started at the school, and he'd already been in a couple of commercials. If Tara wanted to meet Josh, I would introduce her to Josh.

As I headed off to do her bidding, it occurred to me that I was acting more and more like a willing toady, rushing to obey my master's whim. I should shake hands with Igor, I thought, the vile assistant of Dr. Frankenstein. Or better yet Renfield, the mad, bug-eating lackey of Count Dracula.

But I had it easier than them. Igor had to dig up bodies for the terrible Dr. Frankenstein. My bodies were right there, walking the well-tended grass of our school. And all I had to do with them was introduce them to Tara.

But I realized something that both of those henchmen must have realized, too. I was starting to enjoy it.

As I approached Josh, a strange sense of hunger came over me, almost making me drool. Hunger for what, I didn't know, but I found myself rubbing my hands together like a fly preparing to dine. All the while, my two twists of hair both dangled to the left side of my face, feeling eerily heavy and off center. Like the hunch on Igor's back must have felt to him.

I had started taking lunch in the library, not eating—not even feeling hungry. And anyway, by taking the time to do my homework during lunch, I avoided thinking too much and seeing all the strange eating behaviors that had begun to plague more and more students in the school. It was beyond just weird. It was, in fact, so disturbing, my whole body shuddered when I thought about it. I had always been pretty talented at blocking out things that I didn't want to think about. Now was one of those times when such a skill came in very handy.

I was sitting there, working hard at blocking everyone and everything out when Freddy and Danté noisily barged into the library, to the librarian's dirty looks. They spotted me right away.

"Yo, Parker!" said Freddy. "More curls? What's up with *that?*"

I didn't answer him. I just stared at him. Through him.

"Let it go," Danté said to Freddy, sitting at my table. "He's in one of his moods."

One of my moods? I thought. *Since when do I have moods?*

"Sorry," I said. "I was somewhere else for a second. What's up?"

"Did you hear about Ernest?"

"What about him?"

"He hasn't been in school for days," Freddy said. "Geez, Parker, didn't you even notice that?"

I shook my head. "What's wrong with him?"

"That's the thing," said Danté, pulling his chair closer. "No one knows."

Freddy nodded. "First it was just the way he was acting . . . you know, like he was tired all the time."

"Big deal," I said.

"Yeah, but now it's ten times worse. It's like someone tweaked his meds, or something. Or maybe he got tackled one too many times."

"Anyway," says Danté, "it turns out that it's not just in his head. The story going around is that he has some kind of bizarre bone condition—his entire body is hardening."

"What?!"

"His parents took him to a special clinic halfway across the country," Danté added, "where he can be studied."

I shivered and tried to shake the feeling off. "You don't know if any of that's true—it could be all talk."

"Could be." Freddy shrugged. "But I believe it. Did you see how pasty his skin looked his last days here?"

"Yeah," said Danté. "And all he did was drink milk, like he couldn't get enough of the stuff."

". . . Calcium," I heard myself say in a voice so hollow, so empty, I barely recognized it as my own. "You need calcium to grow bone. . . ." And I started to think about all the other strange appetites. Mud. Rocks. What was in that stuff? I took geology—I knew. Silicon, iron. If Ernest's body was building bone, what could a human being possibly be building with silicon or iron?

I stood up and walked away.

"Hey," Freddy said, "where you going?"

His voice faded into the distance. I ran to the bike racks, jumped on my motorbike, and rode it home. My mind was whirling the whole way.

When I got home, Garrett was in the living room, on the sofa, watching TV.

That was the first time I had ever seen him just watching TV. Garrett was always kind of hyper. Usually, if he wasn't playing a video game, he was in his room playing his guitar, or in the garage waxing his car, or doing something active. He wasn't someone who sat and watched TV in the middle of the afternoon.

"Hey, Garrett," I said, with more care, more sincerity than I had ever shown for him, "you're home from school early."

Garrett turned to me. "So are you." His skin was very, very pale.

"Yeah. Well. So, are you feeling okay?"

"Yeah," he said. "I'm fine. Just a little tired." He turned back to the TV.

A straight answer with no insult? Something was very wrong. I walked over to him, pretending I was interested in the old re-run he was watching, and glanced down at him. His skin wasn't just pale; it was gray, like an old tombstone. I turned to catch his eyes. They had always been brown, like mine. But now they were turning gray, too. Cloudy gray, like cataracts.

I turned and left the room, a feeling of horror growing in the pit of my stomach.

Whatever Ernest had, Garrett had it as well, and I'd bet that all those other weird-acting kids in school had also contracted the same strange sickness.

Then a thought arose—a thought I had always been able to push away, but now it clawed to the surface of my mind. It was the terrible knowledge that there was one thing Ernest and Garrett had in common.

They had both spent time with Tara.

"Maybe she's a werewolf," Katrina said.

"Don't be stupid," I told her. "Tara is no such thing." I was out in the backyard, skimming leaves from the pool, while Katrina sat on a lounge chair cuddling Nasdaq, our disinterested Siamese cat, who would have rather been anywhere else than on Katrina's lap at that moment.

"Have you ever seen her on a full moon?" said Katrina. "Besides, she comes from some weird foreign place. That's where werewolves come from."

I pulled the long pool skimmer up and purposely swung it over the lounge chair so that it dripped water on Katrina. Nasdaq took off, and Katrina just yelled at me.

"For your information," I told Katrina, "I *have* seen her on the full moon, and she did not change into a wolf—or anything else—so your theory is all wet." I shook the pool skimmer over her again to emphasize the point.

"All right," said Katrina. "So maybe she's a ghost."

"Ghosts have no substance," I reminded her. "You can't touch a ghost—and I've touched her. She's no ghost."

"Well, then she's an alien, or a zombie, or a robot." Katrina was just reaching now, and we both knew it. Finally, she gave up with a sigh.

I wanted to totally drench Katrina for saying those things, but I couldn't, because deep down I knew that she was onto something. Certainly Tara wasn't the things Katrina had suggested, but she wasn't what she pretended to be, either.

11
SMASHING HISTORY

I believe that we have free will. I believe we get the chance to make choices in our lives. Not everything is set in stone from the moment we're born. We choose our destiny, our ultimate fate. But I also think that we don't realize the choices we've made until after we make them. We're racing down a freeway, only to realize we've missed all the exits, and the only direction we can go is dead ahead.

I might have been able to choose a different path after the first twisted curl appeared on my head—even after the second one. But by the time Tara reached up into my hair that third time, gently curling my hair around her finger and leaving behind a twitching, living thing, a part of me knew deep down that there was no turning back. Choice had become destiny. Future became fate.

She gave me that third lock on a windy Sunday, in the old oil field. Clouds billowed in the sky, high above. The dense cumulus puffs were shredded and re-formed by the fierce, tangling winds. We had started the insectlike oil pumps bobbing. It had become a tradition after that first day she had showed me this place. We would struggle to get them moving and stay until the last of them had ground itself still. Today she had prepared a picnic feast of exotic sliced meats with strange Italian names: mortadella, prosciutto, capocollo.

There were things I had to ask Tara today. I didn't want to ask them, but I had to. I felt there was no going on for me if I didn't have at least some of the answers.

I took a bite of my sandwich. Delicious, I thought . . . but something was missing. Something I couldn't place. It was that way with everything I ate lately. Flavors had less bite; textures were less defined. I took a second bite, and a third, then finally I broke the silence.

"What did you do to Ernest, Tara? What did you do to him, and Garrett, and all the others?"

A gust of wind caught my paper plate, and it tumbled away, pasting itself across the eye of a giant bobbing mantis before blowing off into the trees beyond.

"I don't know what you mean. I didn't lay a hand on them."

And I believed her, because I knew it had nothing to do with her hands. "Garrett said you took your glasses off."

"Of course I did," she said. "It's not like I wear them twenty-four/seven."

"You've never taken them off for me."

She looked straight at me, but made no move to take off her shades. "Is our friendship based on whether or not you can see my eyes?" She smirked, making me feel foolish, but I wasn't going to let that stop me.

"I want you to take off your glasses. I want you to do it now."

"No," she said. Then she spread mustard on her sandwich and gave no further explanation.

I stood up, feeling angry. She could not dismiss me so quickly. Not after I had accepted the task of luring people for her.

"I don't believe your eyes are sensitive to the light. I don't believe what's going on in school has nothing to do with you. And I don't believe you're anything but bad news. I'm out of here." I turned to leave. I got as far as the first oil well, and then she called out to me.

"Please don't go, Parker. I'm sorry. I'm so, so sorry."

Hearing her apologize was enough to stop me. She had never been sorry for anything she had done. She always seemed to move through life with no conscience or regrets. I turned back to her.

"Exactly what are you sorry for?"

"For keeping you in the dark for so long. For all the half-truths and all the times I could have told you but didn't."

She came toward me, but I took a step back. She seemed hurt by that.

"Why can't I see your eyes?" I asked her. "Why won't you let me?"

She sighed. "It's very hard to explain," she told me. "It has to do with the way I look at people. I see very deeply when I look at people. Very few have the strength to look back."

"And what happens when they do?"

"They . . . change."

"That's crazy—you can't change people just by looking at them."

But then I thought, why not? People are changing all the time—changing their minds, their actions, their beliefs. Sometimes it takes an earth-shattering event to do it, but sometimes people change at the drop of a hat. Who's to say that a glance from Tara couldn't alter someone in ways they never imagined?

"Yes, it is crazy," she said. "But it's also true. My gaze sort of . . . hardens people's hearts to the world around them."

Tara looked down. I could sense that all her layers of protection were gone. I'd never seen her vulnerable before. She had always been so sure of herself. I wanted to ask her more. Why was it that those who saw her eyes developed strange cravings for mud and milk? How could something as simple as a glance do that? But there were tears now, seeping out from beneath her sunglasses. When I saw that, I couldn't ask her anything more.

"Do you hate me?" Tara asked. "Do you hate me for who I am?"

"I don't even know who you are," I told her. "How could I hate you?"

She reached her hand toward me. I let her wrap a lock of my hair around her finger. "My eyes are a curse. I move from one place to another with no companions. No friends. I've never really wanted a friend until now, Baby Baer." I could feel the slight pull and tingle as my hair curled tight around her finger. I could feel it transform. I reached up and touched the lenses of her shades: dark silver like a still, summer lake and as smooth as a camera lens.

"Be my friend, Baby Baer. The others who tried to be my friends over the years were always too cold, or their tempers were too hot. But you, Baby Baer—you're just right. Be my friend, forever and ever."

I could feel the weight of the new curling lock on my temple. "I already am your friend," I told her.

She smiled. "Then let me show you something. . . ."

I returned with Tara to her mansion. Her parents were still away, but I was beginning to wonder if she even had parents.

The mansion looked like it always did. Overdone in marble and artwork, spotlessly clean, and the door unlocked. While everyone else in our neighborhood had all kinds of security systems, Tara invited trespassers.

"Don't you worry about all of this stuff getting stolen?" I asked as we stepped in.

"Anyone who wants to take things is welcome. I wouldn't miss any of it, anyway."

"But what if someone tried to kill you?"

"I'd kill them first," she said, like it was nothing. Like it would be so easy for her to do.

Between the kitchen and the ballroom, we came to a large oak door. I remembered this door. It had been open once before, but Tara had quickly closed it. "Nothing in there for you to see," she had told me then. I guess that wasn't quite true, because now this was where we were headed.

She pulled open the door to reveal a set of stone steps heading down into darkness—but instead of going downstairs, she turned to go into the kitchen. "Wait here. I'll be right back."

There was a musty odor rising from the basement: earthy, like a mountain cavern. Cold, damp air breathed out of that doorway, making me rub my arms to stay warm. *But cold air sinks,* I thought, *it doesn't rise.* Yet this strange air was indeed rising from the basement, like a draft fed by an unseen wind.

I was uneasy standing at the head of the steps and glad when Tara returned. She held a candlestick in her hand. The flame flickered in the breeze rising from below. "C'mon," she said. "And don't be afraid."

She began down the stairs, and I followed close behind, not wanting to fall out of the light cast by the candle, thinking about how Danté was afraid of the dark and sympathizing. "Wh-why would I be afraid?"

"Not that you would . . . but you mustn't . . . because if you are, they can sense your fear."

Not even the candlelight made me feel safe now. "They? Who are *they?*"

"You know. The monsters."

I stopped moving. My feet just wouldn't take another step. "What do you mean . . . monsters?"

She said nothing for a moment. Then she laughed. "I'm kidding! Honestly, Baby Baer, you're so gullible!"

"Ha-ha," I said as I caught up with her on the steps. Usually basement stairs were short, but these kept turning corners as they went down.

"Trust me," she said. "There's nothing down here that can hurt you."

"Except for you," I told her.

"Hmm. Good point."

We finally reached the bottom. My eyes had not yet adjusted to the dim light, but I could see well enough to make out shapes around us. "What are those?" I asked.

She reached out her candle and lit a second one in a candle-holder that stood five feet tall. It was gold, but covered in layer after layer of candle drippings. Then she lit another such candle stand and another. Bit by bit the space around us was revealed by the flickering lights of the candles, and I could see what filled Tara's basement.

Statues.

Dozens upon dozens of pale stone statues, like the finest Rodins or Michelangelos, filled every corner of the massive basement. Some of the figures were in robes, likenesses from ancient times. Others were dressed in clothes from Revolutionary or Victorian times. Some wore modern clothes, and others wore no clothes at all. They stood facing in different directions, stares locked on invisible points before them. I had never looked that closely at the ones upstairs, but here, surrounded by so many of them, I couldn't help but be awed by the workmanship. It was their faces that struck me more than anything. The perfect textures. The chiseled wrinkles.

"Tara, these are amazing!"

"I knew you'd like them. My family has been collecting them for ages. There are too many to fit up in the house, so we keep them down here."

We wandered through the maze of figures. They weren't just people, but animals as well: mythical ones—unicorns and griffins. A man with the snarling head of a bull.

"All this must be worth a fortune!"

Tara just shrugged. "It's only worth something if you sell it. These will never be sold." Then she reached behind one of the statues and pulled out something completely out of place. It was a metal baseball bat. She smiled slyly and handed it to me.

"I want you to break them."

I just stood there dumbfounded, the bat dangling from my hand. "What?"

"Break them. It's not that hard. Just swing."

I looked at the stunning works around me. The finely crafted expressions. The details on the hands. "Why would you want me to do that?"

Tara looked around at the statues, and I could hear hatred and disgust as she spoke. "Because these are the only friends I've ever had—stone faces that can't answer back . . . can't show emotion. I'm so tired of them, Parker. I want them gone. I want to start fresh and new. I want you to help me."

"I can't destroy things so beautiful."

"Time will destroy them if you don't. Time destroys everything. But if you destroy them, it will mean something."

"What could it possibly mean?"

She gave me that sly grin again. "You'll see."

I was not much of a vandal. I didn't go around tagging graffiti. I didn't go to the old cemetery and push over tombstones, like some other kids were known to do—but as I held the bat in my hand, I did feel an urge to use it. I had never willfully broken anything in my life, but suddenly I felt a need . . . I felt a *craving* to break something then. Perhaps it wasn't a craving for mud, but it was a craving all the same. It had been so long since I had felt much of anything at all, the craving felt good. Its burning need for satisfaction was, in itself, satisfying.

"What are you angry at, Parker?"

"Nothing."

"I don't believe that. Everyone's angry at something. Reach down. Find it. Bring it to the surface."

It turns out I didn't have to reach down too far. There were quite a lot of things I was angry about. Angry in a grumpy, brooding kind of way. It was the kind of anger that simmers but doesn't boil. But I could make it boil. I could make it bubble, steam, and explode if I wanted to. Knowing I had that power was terrible and wonderful at the same time.

"I'm angry at my parents," I said, "for the way they spend so much time on themselves and so little on us kids."

"What else?"

"I'm angry at my sister. How lousy, rotten, spoiled she is."

"What else?"

I gripped the bat tighter. "I'm angry at my science teacher. The way she expects everything so orderly and perfect."

"And?"

"And the guy at the bicycle store who always rips us off. And the kids at school who think they're so cool. And the basketball coach; and that supermarket checker; and that nasty neighbor; and the lying, cheating sleazeball at the comics store; and—"

Suddenly there were no words. The pot had boiled over with anger. Anger like I had never felt before. It exploded through the tips of my fingers, filling the aluminum bat, and I swung, taking off the head of a Roman soldier. A second swing crumbled his torso, then I turned and swung wildly, tearing loose the wing of a flying horse. Over and over. Sounds bellowed from my mouth—screams of rage. Rage at my life, so comfortable and plastic; rage at the world, so twisted and confusing; rage at the universe, so large and uncaring. I had opened up a doorway in myself that I didn't know existed, and the rage blinded me to everything but the brutal, battering swing of the bat. I turned and swung again and again. Tara had to duck to avoid getting hit as well. Either the stone was softer than marble or I was stronger, or both, because it fractured and crumbled with every swing. Then, at last, with a guttural wail that felt like a war cry, I dropped the bat, and it clattered on the ground.

Fine stone dust settled all around, filling my lungs, sticking to the roof of my mouth, leaving behind a bitter, chalky taste. We were in darkness again. I had smashed the candles, too. I heard the flick of a match, and Tara lit the candle in her hand again, to reveal the ruins. Not a single statue remained. Stone arms, legs, and heads littered the ground. Cold eyes looked up from the ruins. A hundred statues, maybe more—they were all gone. Destroyed by my hand. I must have been at it for the better part of an hour, but it seemed like minutes. I knew my muscles should have been sore from it, but they felt strong. Invigorated. As for the bat, it now lay on the ground, dented and worthless.

I was breathing heavily, but I couldn't catch my breath, because the stone dust kept filling my lungs. My hair was heavy with it. I shook my head to get rid of some of the chalky dust, but then I realized it wasn't dust that made my hair heavy. It was my hair itself.

I reached up to find I now had a full head of twisting curls, and every one of them writhed ever so slowly, like the tentacles of a sea anemone. I was too numb now to feel anything about that, although I knew that I should have felt something.

"There," Tara said. "All better now." Then she reached down into the rubble and picked up a stone hand that had fractured at the wrist and gave it to me, like a trophy for my efforts. "Save this, so you can always remember your triumph today."

I went home in a daze, put the stone hand on my desk, and fell into a sound sleep.

12

Darwin's curve

It takes seven years to change, according to my science teacher. We shed layer after layer of skin; we lose cells each time we go to the bathroom; we breath out our substance with every breath, and after seven years, not a single molecule in our body is the same. You could say we become different people.

Sometimes, though, change comes much faster. It comes like a chemical reaction, like bone dissolving in sulfuric acid. Like the explosive reaction of nitroglycerin. I know it was that way for me.

When I went into school on Monday, it was like I was looking at the world through different eyes. Certain things seemed dull and colorless. The brightly painted mural on the side of the gym looked washed out. The sky, though I knew it was a bright, clear blue, seemed fundamentally gray . . . but the trees, the grass, and the flowers in the garden stood out for me like I was seeing them in a different dimension. It felt like I was perceiving them through a new sense I couldn't understand. It was sharp and not all that pleasant, like coming out of a movie theater into the bright light of day. In this new, strange light, people stood out the most, and I felt a certain craving I couldn't name. While passing between classes I was overwhelmed by this new sense as kids bumped past me in the halls, but I found that not everyone had the same effect on me. There were certain kids who seemed as colorless as the walls and floors. These were the ones who walked more slowly, their eyes cast down. By third period I came to understand that these were also the ones Tara had already befriended. Nils Lundgren, Leticia Hernandez, Josh Weinstein, and a whole lot of others.

At lunch, I felt a strange urge to sit with other kids—kids I barely even knew. I felt a need to "schmooze" the way Tara did. I had always had my own clique and wasn't very social beyond my friends. Now I found myself barging into other kids' conversations, sitting down with them like I'd been invited.

"Hey—you're in my English class, right?" I would say. Or, "That's a cool watch you're wearing." Or, "I still don't get quadratic equations—do you?" Anything to start a conversation. At first they treated me like I was some sort of weirdo, saying things like "Whatever," trying to dismiss me. But I was not dismissed so easily. And soon I became part of whatever conversation the group was having, and they didn't mind. This would have been great. It would have been amazing if it weren't for that glaring change in me; that new, painful sense that pulled me toward them. It made me want to intrude into their lives. I felt I could barge my way into their conversations—even into their homes, sitting in their chairs, eating their food.

Just like Tara.

It wasn't just that—I could sense things about people, too. In some weird way I could sense what they were like on the inside. It's hard to put into words. The closest I can come to explaining it is that some kids kind of felt too hard, while others felt too soft. Then there were other kids who felt . . . well . . . just right. I wanted to ask Tara about it, but at the same time didn't want to talk about it at all.

Tara was in school that day, but she kept her distance. Still, I noticed her noticing me. In all the conversations I shouldered my way into that day, one thing became clear: not a single person met my eyes. They would look away, or at each other, but no one could make eye contact. No one but Danté.

"If you're gonna stare at people like a ghoul, at least smile when you do it."

"Huh?"

It was the start of history. Mr. Usher was late, as usual. Danté sat next to me. "You're staring at people like you want to eat them."

"No, I'm not."

"You are. And by the way . . ." He pointed at my hair. "Your new 'do' is a 'don't.'"

I reached up and brushed the tangled, dangling curls back from my face. I actually liked the way they felt. Like silky, coiled springs.

"Most people like it," I said, not really knowing or caring what most people thought.

"Yeah, whatever."

Then he studied me. He looked at my eyes, then he shivered. "What's happening to you, Parker?"

I answered him honestly. "I'm not sure . . . but I think I kind of like it."

Then he looked away. "Man, if you're gonna stare like that, at least have the decency to hide it." He reached into his backpack and scrounged around for a few seconds until he pulled out an old pair of sunglasses, all scratched and crusty from being in the bottom of his pack. "Here." He tossed them on my desk, and they wobbled themselves still.

I picked them up and slipped them on. Even though they were dark, they didn't change my vision of things at all. They might as well have been clear. But I guess they did hide my eyes. "Better?" I asked.

"Yeah. Now you look just like Tara."

I was unlocking my dirt bike, preparing to go home, when Tara finally came up to me.

"Give me a ride home?" she asked.

"I don't have the extra helmet," I told her.

"It's okay," she said. "I don't need one."

"Everyone needs one," I told her. "It's a law."

"Laws were made for people like them," she said, tossing her gaze toward the many kids funneling out of the school. "Not for us."

The fact that she included me in that statement made me feel both deeply chilled and deeply warm. It was like that with everything nowadays. My life was this jumble of opposites that couldn't possibly fit in the same body, but did. I was feeling terrified, yet somehow I was at peace. Feeling revolted, yet somehow attracted to this strange thing I was becoming.

"What did you do to me?" I asked her.

Tara shook her head. "I didn't do much at all. Most of it was your doing. I just planted a seed in your heart. But you've been making it grow better than I ever thought you would." Then she flicked back her hair, and I found myself doing the same. "So are you giving me a ride, or not?"

"Sure."

I started to put on my helmet, but it hurt when I tried to yank it down over my hair.

"I told you," she said. "You don't need that anymore."

"That's crazy—of course I do." I tried one more time to force the helmet on, then Tara grabbed it away from me and tossed it. But she didn't just toss it, she hurled it. I watched it disappear like a baseball flying over a ballpark fence. No one had the strength to throw something that far.

"How did you—"

She climbed onto the bike. "Let's get going."

And so, with no helmet and no chance of tracking it down, I climbed on the dirt bike, started the engine, and took off. The wind pulled our long tendrils of hair, making them whip out behind us like streamers.

I never expected what Tara did next. It came as a sudden, horrific surprise, so unexpected that I didn't react fast enough to stop it. We were up on Ridgeline Road—the path that led out from the valley into the exclusive neighborhood where we lived.

As we were about to make the turn on Darwin's Curve, right above the deadly cliff, Tara leaned forward, grabbed my hands, and locked her elbows. I tried to turn the handlebars, but couldn't—Tara's grip was too strong.

"What are you doing?!"

"Making a point."

We were heading straight for the gap in the railing!

"Tara, no! Are you nuts?!"

"You're gonna love this, Baby Baer!"

"Nooooo!!"

We hit the edge of the road and were airborne. I screamed, not understanding why Tara had done this. There was nothing beneath us now but a hundred feet of air and the sharp jagged rocks below. The bike fell away first, then I felt Tara's hands slip away from me; and I was alone, falling to a painful, sorry end.

That feeling came—the feeling of the first drop on a roller coaster. The nasty tingle of free fall. Two seconds . . . three seconds . . . then contact!

I hit a jagged rock on my side and bounced off it. My skull connected with another rock, and I went spinning in the other direction, tumbling against the jagged stones, my arms and legs flailing with each impact, bones breaking—shattering—with every boulder I hit. I could feel the force of every single impact, yet no pain accompanied it, and I thought, *Maybe I'll be lucky enough to die before I have to feel the pain.*

But the pain never came.

When I finally came to rest at the bottom of the cliff, my jeans and shirt were torn to shreds —even the soles of my sneakers had been ripped apart, but there wasn't a single scratch on my body. I stood up, flexed my arms, and touched my face. Nothing! No cuts, no bruises, no blood! It was impossible. I had felt my bones break and my flesh tear, yet I showed no signs of the injuries. It was as if I had healed in an instant.

"See, I told you!" Tara came strolling up behind me. "Wanna do it again?"

"No!"

And even if I had wanted to, we couldn't, because a few yards away lay my dirt bike, a useless mass of twisted metal and rubber.

"But how . . . how did . . . how could . . ."

"Shhh," Tara said. "Never ask how." And she winked at me, making me feel like we were in our own special club. A club of two. Secret and superior. You can't imagine how intoxicating that felt.

Never ask how. At that moment, it felt like the wisest advice I had ever gotten.

We walked all the way home and didn't say a word to each other, but that was all right. I took her to her front door, said a simple good-bye, then went home. I didn't even notice if anyone else was home. I think parts of my brain had shut down that afternoon. Maybe it was shock, I don't know, but instead I went straight up to my room, changed out of my shredded clothes, and did my homework like nothing had happened. And when I was done, I went downstairs and sat at the dinner table, eating, not listening or hearing what everyone talked about, ignoring the fact that the food didn't seem to fill me in the least. And when dinner was over, I shot some hoops alone on the court, sinking every single one. And then I went to bed.

Simple. Just like any other evening. Except for the fact that I should have been dead, and I wasn't. *Never ask how.* But if I couldn't die, then "never" seemed like a very long time.

13

▲

new Hungers

I did my best to put the trip off Darwin's Curve out of my mind. Believe it or not, it wasn't all that hard to do, because there were other things more pressing. Like the hunger. It grew with each passing day—it seemed worst when I was at school surrounded by others. It was not a hunger for food—I knew that much. It wasn't a hunger for mud, either—I actually tested that possibility and gagged on it. Deep down I knew I had an appetite for something very different, but I could not figure out what it was.

It was four in the morning, at the end of that strange week. I had woken up famished, as usual, but I knew there was no food in the house that would satisfy my hunger.

When I came downstairs and into the kitchen, I found Garrett sitting there in the dark. I jumped when I turned on the light—I wasn't expecting to see him sitting there, so silent, so still. He had no such reaction, though. He didn't flinch from the light. Even in the dim fluorescents of the kitchen, I could see that the sickly pallor of his skin was getting worse. It had turned grainy, like a photo blown up too large. I wondered how Mom and Dad could see him every day and not notice. Then again, maybe they did but were afraid to say anything—as if speaking it aloud would somehow make it real.

Garrett sat there at the kitchen table with a bowl of cereal in front of him, staring down into the bowl. Grape-Nuts, it looked like.

"Midnight snack?" I asked as I grabbed myself some juice from the fridge.

He didn't move for the longest time. Then he turned his head slightly toward me. "I can't cry, Parker."

It was such a strange thing for him to say—so out of character.

"Wh-why would you want to cry?"

Again it took him a long time to answer, as if moving the thought from his mind to his mouth was like trying to start a freight train.

"The cereal," he finally answered.

"What about it?"

"Look closer."

And so I did. I looked close enough to see that it didn't really look like cereal. Plus, there was no cereal box on the table, just the bowl, a spoon, and the container of milk. Still Garrett stared down into the bowl, not moving. Not crying. But in a moment I discovered he shouldn't have been crying at all. He should have been screaming . . . because the door to the pantry was open just enough to reveal an open ten-pound bag on the floor. A bag of Petfit Kitty Litter.

My stomach heaved, but I drank a huge gulp of orange juice to chase the feeling away.

"Why do I want to eat this, Parker? Why am I so hungry for it? Why? Why?" I could see him working his eyes, trying to make tears come out, but they wouldn't come. "Why don't I feel anymore? Why don't I care?"

"You care enough to know something's wrong," I said to him gently. I put my hand on his, gripping it, hoping to give him comfort. His hand was cold. No, not cold . . . it was . . . room temperature. Like a snake.

"But soon I won't care," he said. "Very soon I won't care at all. It'll be like everything else. I don't care about my grades. I don't care about my friends. I don't care about Mom and Dad. About Katrina. About you. I don't care about myself."

Tara did this to him, I thought. But then something else occurred to me. She had done it *for* me. She had done it because I had been so angry at Garrett that day. And suddenly I knew that Garrett's condition was my fault and my fault alone.

. . . *Na* . . .

I had cursed him, and somehow Tara had followed through on the curse.

"I'm scared," he whispered.

"I know," I told him. "Don't be. It'll be okay."

"No . . . I *want* to be scared. It's a *feeling.* I want to hold on to that feeling. Please, Parker. Please let me be scared. *Help* me to be scared. . . ."

It went against every fiber in my body, but I had to respect his wishes, and so I dug down as deep as I could to find something that would keep him scared. All I had to do was tell him the truth, based on what I had heard about Ernest.

"It's going to get worse," I told him. "Your bones are going to get thicker. Your joints are going to grow stiff, and no doctors will be able to figure out what's wrong. The only good thing about it is that you won't be able to feel how much you're suffering."

He blinked. His lids went slowly down, then slowly up. Not a bit of moisture slipped from his glazed, graying eyes.

"Are you scared, Garrett?" I asked.

Garrett breathed in. Garrett breathed out. "Not enough, bro. Not enough."

We sat there in silence for a good ten minutes. Then finally he said, "Go back to bed, Parker." And so I did. Just before I left, I turned to catch sight of him lifting his spoon to his mouth, eating the kitty litter. I went to my bed, put my head beneath my pillow, and I began to cry. I cried for both of us.

I couldn't get back to sleep. My head was full of thoughts as twisted as Tara's twirling locks. As twisted as my own. Before dawn I decided to do something about it.

I went to the bathroom. I didn't look in Garrett's room, because I didn't want to know if he was there or still downstairs having his fancy feast. I remembered that there was a pair of scissors in a drawer still childproofed from when Katrina was small. I reached in, undid the latch, and pulled out the scissors. As I raised them toward my head, my curls pulled back. It was more than a twitch. It was a squirm. I could see the eerie way they moved.

With the scissors shaking in my hand, I caught one of the curls between the blades and began to snip.

Until that moment, I had never known the meaning of pain. I once broke my leg in two places while snowboarding. I once had a root canal. I once took a softball thrown at full force, in the most tender spot known to man. But none of those things came anywhere close to the pain I felt as the jaw of the scissors came down on that first thick tendril.

The pain shot through my scalp, zigged through my brain, and clasped my spine like barbed wire. I could no longer feel my arms, my legs, my body. It was all the pain I *should* have felt when I fell from Darwin's Curve. I was blinded. There was nothing left of me but the pain. Then the pain began to fade.

I found myself curled up in the fetal position, knees to chest, between the toilet and bathtub, the scissors lying on the floor beside me. But something was wrong with them. They didn't look right, and as my vision came into focus, I could see that one of the blades had snapped.

I stood up slowly, balancing against the sink to keep my knees from buckling beneath me. The twisting, snaking curls were still there—all of them—and in the sink was the broken scissor blade.

After that, I slunk back to my room. The sun was rising now, but I didn't feel like facing the day. I crawled into bed and fell asleep, and although I knew I had vivid and bleak nightmares, I didn't dare remember any of them.

Somewhere between 5:30 A.M. and noon, Tara claimed her next victim.

14
▲
THE SCULPTOR

I woke up at noon, still feeling profoundly void in my mind and in the pit of my stomach. It was Saturday; my parents were off at the country club, Dad playing golf, Mom organizing yet another social function. I slithered down the stairs. I couldn't find Garrett, but Katrina was there, sitting in the living room, brushing Nasdaq. There was something off about the way she did it. Not so much rhythmically as mechanically. My heart missed a beat. I slowly approached her.

"Hey, Katrina," I said. "What's up?"

"You're right," Katrina said.

"Right about what."

"She's not a vampire. She's something else." Katrina continued to brush the cat, and the cat clearly didn't like it.

"What did you do?"

"I went to her house and snuck in." Katrina shivered.

"What happened?" I demanded. "Did something happen when you were there?"

"She caught me snooping. She . . ."

"Her glasses! She didn't take off her glasses, did she? Please, Katrina, tell me she didn't take off her glasses!"

"No," Katrina said.

I breathed a deep and thankful sigh of relief.

"No. She didn't have to take them off. She wasn't wearing them."

Gooseflesh rose on my arms and legs, and I felt my dangling curls start to squirm, their roots like deep weeds in my brain and spine. "Did you see her eyes?"

Katrina turned her gaze to me. The cat bolted from her lap. "Those things aren't eyes," Katrina said. "There's forever in there. . . ."

I stormed to Tara's mansion. I didn't know what I would do when I got there, but I couldn't just sit idly by and watch my brother, then my sister, fall victim to her as so many already had. How long would it take for Katrina? I wondered. It had taken two weeks until Ernest had been carted away to be a textbook case of some strange new disease. About the same amount of time passed before Garrett lost all sense of emotion and chowed down on kitty litter. What kind of future did Katrina have now? No future at all.

Tara's door was unlocked. It was always unlocked. What did she have to fear? I swung the door wide and stepped in. "Tara," I shouted. "I want to talk to you!"

There was no answer. I took a few more steps into the house.

"Tara!" I called again, even louder. "Are you here?"

My voice echoed through the mansion, bouncing off walls in faraway rooms, only to return unanswered.

I walked into the living room and sat down in a chair with thick, swallowing cushions, prepared to wait until she came back. I didn't care how long it took. My mind was filled with fury and confusion, the feelings pulling me deeper into myself. I don't know how long I sat there, seething, not moving a muscle. It felt like time was no longer moving at the usual speed, as if time had become strangely elastic and unpredictable. Was this another effect of my "change"? I thought. Freedom from the laws of time?

I can't say that I finally calmed down exactly, but at some point my eyes focused on my surroundings. It almost felt like I was waking up as I remembered where I was. I was sitting in Tara's living room, uninvited and alone.

As my eyes swept the room, they kept returning to one of Tara's paintings on the wall. It was a huge stone building, an ancient place, with gigantic columns all the way around holding up the roof. It stood high on a hill, overlooking a city.

I stood up and walked closer to the painting. The columns looked like they were made out of marble, turned pink and gold by the setting sun. The gigantic roof was made of stone, too, with intricate carvings on the sides. Between the columns, I could make out a large golden statue of a woman.

It was beautiful, but I was hardly in the mood for art appreciation now. Then an uneasy realization began to snake its way inside my head.

I had seen this building before.

Tara had told me she had done all of her paintings on her travels around the world. She painted places she had been, things she had seen . . . but I had seen this building before, in a photograph. It was famous. Only . . .

I raced out of Tara's house and headed home. Maybe I was wrong about this; maybe I was imagining things, but I had to find out.

I ran into my house, then up to my room, grabbed my backpack, and dug through it until I found my world history textbook, a big old thing that weighed my pack down like lead—I guess to remind us how much world history there was. I flipped it open and quickly shuffled through the pages until I came to what I was looking for. Chapter 12, Section 3. Ancient Greece. It was a photograph of the Parthenon, high on a hilltop in Greece, built around 440 B.C. to be the temple of Athena, a Greek goddess. It was the same building as in Tara's painting, no question about it. Same shape, same columns, same hill. *But now the building was an ancient ruin.* The roof had caved in, the marble columns were broken and battered, and the carvings on the sides of the roof were gone, along with the golden statue.

If Tara painted only the things she had seen . . . just how old was she?

I felt my heart freeze as impossible thoughts raced through my mind. Impossible, like surviving a deadly crash. Impossible, like immortality. I felt unsteady on my feet as the reality of her—and now my—immortality finally hit me. My textbook fell from my fingers and began a long, slow fall to the floor. Time was changing again, but I forced my mind to wrestle it back into a steady pace. By the time the book hit the ground, time appeared to be normal once again.

I wobbled over to the window, and a glint of reflected sunlight caught my eye. I looked down and saw something gleaming in the backyard.

My statue.

The replica of me, in bronze.

It was a work of art, created by an artist. Tara's painting was also a work of art, and it could be explained just as easily. I probably had misunderstood her. Tara didn't just paint what she had seen—she must have painted what she *imagined* it had looked like when it was still intact. Or maybe she had copied it from a book. Sure. That's all. But . . .

I glanced across the room and saw the stone hand on my dresser, the one Tara had given me as a souvenir of my rampage through her basement. Tara's painting wasn't the only unsettling work of art in her house. The statues troubled me just as much.

As I looked down at the bronze sculpture in the backyard, an idea came to me. I grabbed the stone hand off my dresser and slipped it into my backpack.

Michael Fisher, Sculptor.

The next day, while my parents were out, I rifled through their things until I found the receipt in my dad's filing cabinet. My eyes widened at the price they had paid for my statue, but that's not what I was interested in. I just needed the address. It turned out that Michael Fisher's studio wasn't very far away.

It was in a part of town I hardly ever visited—the industrial side, just over the bridge and past the cemetery. It was 7:00 P.M. when I got there. The sun was already below the horizon, and the sky was slipping into darkness. The warehouses and factories were so deserted on a Sunday night, you'd think it was a ghost town. I thought I'd come up with a dark studio and a padlocked door. Lucky for me this artist kept unusual hours. I found Michael Fisher's studio on a block with a scrap yard, a transmission-repair shop, and a bar called Rocky's.

The studio was in a corrugated-steel warehouse, with a huge sliding door to get very large things in and out. The sliding door was partly open, and beyond it I could hear the nasty whine of some sort of machine. I peered inside. A big man stood there, hard at work. He wore a thick black apron and heavy work goggles. The whine was coming from a chain saw that he was using to attack a huge block of wood—and when I say *attack,* I really mean that. He sculpted that wood like he was taking chunks out of an enemy. Sawdust and wood chips flew in every direction.

I stood there and watched, fascinated, as he hacked away with the chain saw until the block of wood began to resemble a crouching human form. He turned off the saw, put it down, then stepped back to admire his work.

"Wow," I couldn't help saying.

The sculptor snapped his eyes toward me, lifting up his goggles to get a better look. Then he wiped his forehead on his sleeve. He said nothing. I took a step inside. Still he said nothing. Just watched me. I'd guess he was about sixty. What little gray hair he had left he wore back in a ponytail, and his nose looked like it had been broken twice, once in each direction. He looked more like a trucker than an artist.

"I can see you're busy," I said, "but I was hoping I could ask you a few questions. About art."

"Art who?" he said, then laughed at my clueless expression. He reached over to his worktable and picked up a water bottle. As he stretched out his arm, his sleeve hiked up, and I could see that from his wrist up, his skin was covered with tattoos.

"Hey, I know you," he said. "Basketball player in bronze. Last name Baer, right?"

"That's me."

"The new hairstyle threw me, but I never forget a face I sculpt. That was a tough sculpture. Your folks are very particular about what they want."

"Yeah, tell me about it," I said.

"Mike Fisher," he said, stepping forward and shaking my hand. My hand nearly disappeared in his. I also noticed that his hand was strangely misshapen. There were lumps at each of his knuckles. Arthritis. I had seen it before on my grandmother's hands, but on these huge hands it was chilling.

"I'm Parker. Parker Baer," I said, trying not to look at his hand.

"So what did you think of my sculpture of you?"

"I loved it," I said.

He shook his head and stared at me, his dark eyes seeming to pierce me. "I hate it when people lie to spare my feelings," he growled.

I sighed. "It took me by surprise," I said. "I didn't know what to make of it."

His eyes softened, slightly. "When your parents commissioned the work, I thought it was about the strangest idea for a birthday present I'd ever heard."

I nodded, and he laughed very suddenly and much too loud.

"Not that I was about to turn them down," he added. "Money's money."

He grabbed a towel and rubbed it all over his face and neck, wiping off the sweat. I glanced around the studio. The place was dark and untidy. Tools, rags, and work materials were scattered on every surface. Sawdust, stone chips, and metal shavings covered the floor.

Unfinished works surrounded us. I saw the top half of a perfectly formed woman who seemed to be growing out of a chunk of stone; there were body parts made of clay lying on benches and several abstract iron sculptures as well. It looked like Michael Fisher was a master sculptor in wood, stone, and metal.

"They're beautiful," I said.

"Beauty isn't the point," he grunted, dropping the towel. "Truth is."

I brushed past a small tree trunk on the floor. I had assumed it was just another piece of wood that he was going to carve, but when I touched it I realized it was made out of stone.

"This is amazing," I said. "This might be your best sculpture of all. It looks exactly like a real piece of wood, down to the tiny cracks in the bark."

Mike laughed out loud, then said, "I can't take credit for that one. It *is* a real piece of wood. Petrified wood. I'm going to use it in my next piece."

I'd read about petrified wood, but I'd never actually seen any. It's the fossilized remains of prehistoric trees. Millions of years ago it was ordinary wood, but over time, water and minerals seeped into and around the wood's cells, eventually replacing them, turning it into a perfect stone replica . . .

. . . which raised a question in my mind.

"How long does it take for wood to petrify?" I asked.

Mike shrugged. "Thousands, maybe tens of thousands of years."

I knew this line of questioning was about to become a runaway train I didn't want to be on. I just kept hoping that I was on the wrong track.

"Is there any way something can turn to stone . . . faster?" I asked.

Mike thought about it. "Not that I can think of," he said finally. Then he added, "Outside of myth and legend, that is."

A runaway train. I tensed for the crash.

"What myths and legends?"

"There are plenty of them. There's the legend of the cockatrice, a monster with the head of a rooster and the tail of a dragon whose glance could turn anyone to stone. Then there's the story of King Midas—a greedy king who was granted his wish that anything he touched turn to gold. He was delighted, until he got hungry. Then anything he tried to eat or drink turned to gold before he could swallow it."

He scratched his chin thoughtfully. "And of course, there's the most famous one of all . . . Medusa. You know the myth of Medusa, don't you?"

I shook my head. Ancient myths of dead civilizations had never seemed especially relevant. Not until recently.

"Medusa was one of three Gorgon sisters. She took the form of a hideously ugly woman, with monstrous teeth and sharp claws. But even worse was her hair. Her head was covered with hissing snakes. She was so terrible to look at, that anyone who caught her gaze was turned into stone. She lived by herself in a dark cave surrounded by statues of men, women, and animals— only they weren't statues at all, of course. They had been her victims. In the end, she got her head cut off by a hero, name of Perseus."

"But none of that is real," I said, wondering if the sudden tightness in my voice sounded as strange to his ears as it did to mine. "I mean, it's only a myth, right?"

"Well," said Mike thoughtfully, "that's the question, isn't it? Personally, I believe that every myth has some nugget of truth at its core. Over the centuries, the story may have changed and become distorted, but somewhere back in the distant past, who knows?"

I reached into my backpack and took out the broken stone hand. My own hand was shaking so much I almost dropped it.

"Can you tell me who made this?" I asked. "Or tell me where it came from, when it was made . . . or at least what kind of stone it is?"

Mike reached forward and took the stone hand from me. His face didn't change, but I could see his eyes registering the quality of the work.

"Very nice," he said. "Very lifelike. Where did you get it?"

"From a friend."

"Where did they get it?"

"That's what I want to find out."

He hefted it in his hand, rubbing his thumb along the broken wrist and the curve of the fingers. "Strange. I've been carving stone for nearly four decades. I can usually tell just by looking what kind of stone it is—and sometimes even which quarry it came from—but this one I don't recognize at all."

He walked over to another workbench against the far side of his studio. I followed. He had more tools on this bench, smaller ones—picks and files, forceps, clamps. And a large magnifying glass.

Mike held the hand under a bright work light and peered at it through the magnifying glass for a full minute, closely studying the rough surface of the break at the wrist.

"Okay," he said at last, "okay." Then he nodded at me and said, "Time to get out the big guns."

He walked over to a deep, cluttered closet, rummaged through it, and finally pulled out an old, rusty microscope. He blew off some dust and wiped the lens with his shirt. "Live long enough and you have one of everything," he said. "I haven't had to use this baby since some rich kook hired me to engrave Shakespearean sonnets on grains of sand during the seventies. What you might call microsculpture."

Mike picked up a tiny steel pick and pointed it at the broken edge of the wrist, scraping off a small sample. He picked up one of the crumbs with a pair of tweezers and put it on a glass slide, then slipped the slide under the microscope. Peering through the eyepiece, he quickly twirled a knob to focus it.

"Hmm . . ." he said. I could see his forehead crinkling with thought. "Hmm," he said again. He straightened up and turned to me. "I'm no geologist, but I know this is something you don't see every day. Take a look."

I bent over the microscope. I squinted and could clearly see the tiny little flake of stone, now magnified to the size of a boulder. Light glinted off the nearly translucent edges, creating a little rainbow effect.

"It almost doesn't look like stone," Mike said. "The structure is very unusual—it doesn't look like a mineral matrix; it looks more like a cellular structure."

I straightened up and looked at him. "Petrified flesh . . . like petrified wood?"

"Flesh doesn't petrify. It rots."

He picked up the stone hand again, along with the large magnifying glass, and held it under the bright light on the worktable. He examined the back of the hand, looking closely at the texture around the knuckles, the wrinkles in the skin. "I don't know who the sculptor was, but this is the most lifelike work I have ever seen."

Then he turned the hand over and let out a low whistle. He looked at me, looked at the hand again, then to me once more. He saw something. Something major. I could tell, because his expression was hard, but also a little bit frightened.

"Tell me about this friend of yours," he said.

"In a minute," I told him. "First, tell me what you see."

He considered it for another moment, then said, "It's something I have never seen in a sculpture before. I can't even imagine how it was done—or why."

"What is it?" I could feel my curls begin to twitch.

He held the hand and the magnifying glass closer to me so I could see. His arthritic fingers shook. They hadn't been shaking before. Even though I didn't want to look, I forced myself.

"Do you see?" he asked, holding the lens over the tips of the stone fingers.

I nodded, unable to speak.

The stone hand had fingerprints.

15

"Here, KITTY KITTY"

I told the sculptor everything I knew about Tara, and everything I suspected. He took me far more seriously than I thought he would. He said he'd go do some research on his own.

It was past eight o'clock when I got home—only I didn't go home. I knew my parents would get on my case for being out and not letting them know where I was . . . that is, if they even noticed I was gone at all. I passed my house and headed straight for Tara's.

All her lights were out. Either she could see in the dark, or no one was home. For all I knew she *could* see in the dark and had eyes in the back of her head. Anything was possible now. Anything. I didn't like the feeling. I was used to a world where a clear line was drawn between improbable and impossible . . . and losing that line was like having no guardrail on Darwin's Curve. There was nothing to keep me from falling off the edge.

I walked down the path to her front door, then turned the knob and let myself in. Even though the house was completely dark, I had a sense of where everything was. I didn't need the light to move effortlessly around obstacles; I was tuned in to their presence. It was weird. . . . No, I was weird. I had a sense beyond sight now, and I knew instinctively that my hair held some new sensory organ. They were *of* me, and yet *not* of me: foreign and familiar at once, like tubular cancer growths—inoperable and rooted so deep in my nervous system, there was no telling where I ended and they began.

Tara wasn't in the house. Instead, I found her out back, swimming laps in the moonless darkness. I stood there, rooted to the spot, waiting for her to acknowledge me, but she didn't. She knew I was there—I could sense it, but still she swam. It was like this wordless communication was taking place between us that I was only dimly aware of. A part of me was speaking to her in a language I didn't know. Yet.

Finally, she stopped swimming, and came over to the edge where I stood. She looked straight at me, but in the darkness I saw nothing but the shadows of her eye sockets. I'm sure she knew that.

"Want to come in for a swim, Baby Baer?" she said. "The water's perfect."

"Perfect like the Mediterranean Sea?" I asked.

She chuckled. "The Mediterranean Sea was never perfect. That's just a myth."

"A myth . . . like you?"

"I was never a myth," she said. "Although people tend to believe I am."

"And what about Perseus?" I asked. "Was he a myth?"

She didn't even flinch at the question. "Oh, Perseus was real, all right—but he wasn't quite the hero legends make him out to be. He didn't cut off my head, for instance, as you've probably figured out. Sure, he tried, but he couldn't resist looking into my eyes—believing himself too powerful to be turned to stone. One look at me, and it was over. He turned to stone with his sword still in his hand. I was so angry, it took only seconds—it can happen that fast, if you're angry enough." Then she smiled. "He was a handsome statue. That is, until you smashed him with a baseball bat."

I suppressed a shiver. "You're supposed to be ugly."

"More lies. Am I ugly to you?"

"No . . . but what you do . . . turning people to stone—it's impossible. . . ."

She pulled herself out of the water, grabbed her robe, and wrapped herself in it. Her hair, I noticed, didn't even appear wet. "Is it so impossible? If you put a person in the ground, they turn to dirt. If you put them in a fire, they turn to ash."

"That's different. . . ."

"Not really. I simply do it in a different way than nature does. I harden their hearts; I harden their minds. Their flesh has no choice but to turn to stone as well."

I stood there, trying to keep the world from spinning as I spoke to her. Nothing seemed real anymore. In the darkness nothing even seemed solid. "Why?" I asked. "Why would you want to turn people to stone? What purpose could it possibly serve?"

She looked at me as if she didn't understand the question. "It's just . . . what I do."

"You mean to say you just do it because you *can?*"

"No! I do it because I *must*. Humans must breathe; humans must eat or they die. And I must turn flesh to stone. Every time someone hardens—every time someone's skin goes cold and solid from my gaze, I grow stronger," she said, with a grin that I could feel more than see.

"Why here? Why our town?"

"Do you really have to ask? Look at your school—look at all of your rich friends. If there's anything I've learned, it's that wealth hardens people. Turning them to stone is easy—they're already halfway there before I start."

She was right. If love of money is the root of all evil, then having money is the root of all boredom. When you can have everything, you find there's nothing you really want. When you can do anything, you find there's nothing you really care to do. You become lazy. Life feels like a boulder you don't want to lift. How much would it have taken to turn me to stone, if Tara had wanted to when she first met me? *Halfway there.* I knew exactly what she meant.

Tara looked at me. Even though I couldn't see her eyes, I could feel her looking deep, deep into the very center of my being. I felt myself being examined, and probed, and weighed.

"I know all this is hard for you, but it will soon get easier. I think you're ready."

I didn't want to ask the question, but I had to. Even though I already knew the answer, I had to hear it from her lips.

"Ready for what?"

And, as usual, her answer surprised me. "I'm lonely, Parker.

You have no idea how lonely. I've been around the world twelve dozen times, and I've blended into any culture I chose. Yet in all that time, in all those places, no matter how many people surrounded me, I've always been alone."

"What about your sisters?"

She laughed. It was an ugly sound. "Typical dysfunctional family. I can't stand them."

I had to let out a sick little chuckle myself. Three flesh-turning Gorgon sisters. What could be more dysfunctional than that?

"I was alone by choice," she continued. "The people around me meant nothing to me. Looking at them was like looking at . . . food. I never realized what I was missing, until I met you."

I didn't know whether to be flattered or terrified. "What's so special about me?"

She shrugged. "I guess you were just in the right place at the right time. I was ready for a true friend, and you were there." Then she giggled. "Or maybe I just like your eyes."

"My eyes don't turn people to stone," I told her.

She whispered, ". . . They could if you let them." She stood there a moment longer, then she turned and went inside without looking back.

"But . . . but why would I want to? Why would I *ever* want to?"

She gave no answer. Instead, she closed the door, leaving me alone in the dark yard.

Another sleepless night. I suspected I was no longer a creature that needed sleep. I was so much like her already. I hated it; I loved it. I felt strong, but I felt powerless. What was I? Who was I now? Tara had given me the gift and curse of being like her—immortal—but at what price? Would I now be a predator, like her?

I tried to reason with myself, rationalizing to make all this easier to swallow. Perhaps I didn't have to be like her. Perhaps there were other ways to satisfy a medusan hunger. The night moved on ever slower, until I lost patience with it, and suddenly I felt myself PUSHING time, making it move at a pace that pleased me, until dawn finally broke.

My decision was made now. I knew I was already past the point of turning back, because Tara had already changed me—but I would not live like her, growing strong by turning humans to stone.

As I walked down the stairs, I could feel a tingly lift in my step. I felt more alive than I had ever felt in my life. I was completely tuned in to my surroundings. I felt like I belonged exactly where I was, doing exactly what I was doing. It was a feeling I had never experienced in my life. *It comes from accepting what you are,* I heard a voice say in my head. *Accepting what you've become.* I could tell you it was Tara's voice in my head, but I'd be lying, because I knew the voice was my own.

I walked to the kitchen, my tightly curled locks picking up the vibrations of everything around me. Walls were flat and featureless waves; the upholstered chairs were soft hills in the plane; the steel-and-glass coffee table was a sharp, angular spike.

The houseplants, though, were different. They were alive. I could feel the life force coming from them. I moved closer and inhaled it, drank it in. It was delicious, but empty. It was like smelling a grilled steak, but not being able to eat it. Only now did I realize how hungry I was, but it wasn't food I was hungry for.

I knew at once that no one was home. Other than the plants, I could feel no other life force in the house. . . . No, that wasn't true. . . . In a distant room, near the back of the house, under Katrina's bed, I was aware of a small life.

Nasdaq.

I wanted the cat to come to me, but I wondered if he would. Would he sense that I had changed? Would he hiss at me, the hair on his back standing on end? Would he recognize me for what I was?

"Nasdaq . . ." I said softly.

He heard—even from so far away, he heard. I knew he would. I felt him stretch and stand up. The day before yesterday, I knew, he would never have been able to hear me, and even if he had, he would have ignored me. But not today.

I could feel Nasdaq approaching, down the hall. I was becoming irresistible. Like Tara.

"Here, kitty kitty," I said, snickering at the old line. Nasdaq padded around the corner and slinked into the room, rubbing the side of his body against my leg. He purred, delighted, longing to be closer to me. To be enfolded in my arms.

I obliged. I leaned over and put my hands under his stomach and chest, supporting him as I lifted him to my lap. "Hi, Nasdaq," I said pleasantly, looking at him. "You like me like this? Yes, you do. I can see it. I can see it in your eyes."

I was looking directly into his eyes now, and he didn't look away. I could feel his muscles stiffen slightly, but he didn't resist.

I could feel the moment that I triggered the change. It was like flicking a switch deep within the cat's brain. It would take time for his entire body to be transformed, but the damage was already done. There was no stopping it now.

I found that my vision had gone dark, and as it came back, I became aware of the hardening body of the cat in my lap. A stiffening of bone, then ligaments. A seizing of flesh. Nasdaq turned to stone while I held him, from the center out. He didn't seem to care. Neither did I. I felt neither pity nor guilt for what I had done. And the decision to do it—was it a decision at all? The desire to turn him to stone had been as irresistible as a sneeze, or scratching an overwhelming itch. Having done it, I felt stronger now . . . but only a little. It was the slightest taste of power, and gave me an appetite for more. I put the stone cat down beside the fireplace, already knowing that my hunger wouldn't stop there. The stone-turning urge had grabbed me now, and as much as I tried to deny it, something as tiny as a cat was not nearly enough to satisfy it.

I put on my shades before I left the house. Not the cruddy ones Danté had given me—those had broken in the fall from Darwin's Curve. I had a new pair now—sleek and expensive.

I walked to school that morning, cutting through the woods, rather than following the road. I caught sight of every creature I could on the way. Stone crows plunged from tree limbs. Geckos—dozens of geckos—solidified on the rocks on which they perched. Just like the one Tara had given me. A skunk turned so quickly, it didn't have the chance to spray. The urge still raged. Each creature turned to stone was a kernel feeding the hunger. Like a single cereal flake in an empty bowl. How many flakes would it take until my stone-turning urge was satisfied? Would this be my life now? Foraging forests for small animals? There was only one thing I could do. I didn't want to, but I didn't see any way around it.

I had to find bigger animals.

16
▲
SOMEBODY'S BEEN
SITTING IN MY CHAIR

You can't imagine what it's like to see the world through a new sense. It is overpowering, thrilling, and terrifying all at once. I couldn't catch my breath or slow the beating of my heart. Walls meant nothing, because I could feel life right through them. I felt I could walk through those walls if I wanted to, as if they were made of tissue paper. Turning Nasdaq to stone had made this new sense much stronger.

I flipped my head to let the wind sift through my curls. They were like antennae tuning in to vibrations of everything alive. Before I really knew what I was doing, I found myself wandering up the driveway of a house a few streets away from mine. I don't even remember having walked there. The people who lived here had left their front gate unlocked. As I stepped through the gate, I sensed a gardener behind a hedge—a bright pattern of life shone through, even though I couldn't see him. I felt hungry, but I steered clear of him, not wanting to be caught.

The idea of personal property is a myth!

That's what Tara had said—but that's not what she meant. Now I understood what she meant. There's no such thing as *other people's* property, because right now I felt like everything was mine. And so it felt perfectly natural to turn the knob of the front door and walk in.

I knew exactly where everyone in the house was. I didn't have to hear them; I sensed them, so staying out of their path was easy. I went into the kitchen. There was a cherry pie cooling on the counter. I dug my hand into it, taking a big juicy scoop. It was like I had no sense of remorse or responsibility. I would never have done something so weirdly selfish before, but suddenly old rules didn't apply. I pawed the hunk of pie into my mouth like a bear scooping honey. Usually cherry pie is my favorite, but not anymore. Taste was nothing compared to this new sense. I spat the flavorless pie into the sink and wiped my hands on a dish towel.

I went into the family room next. The TV was on. Children's cartoons. I sensed the child exactly fourteen feet away, in the bathroom—yet a sense of life lingered in a small chair near the TV. I sat in it, soaking in those traces of life the way, in an earlier time, I would have enjoyed the aroma of that cherry pie. I was too big for the chair, and the legs beneath me snapped. I left the chair in ruins on the floor. I didn't care. These things of the world were not important to me anymore.

I moved through the house, focusing on the traces of life I found. Bedrooms were the best, I suppose because that's where people spend a third of their lives. I never realized how much life we leave behind. The beds had all been neatly made; this was a house of tidy people. I tested the beds. In one, the traces of life seemed hard. Old. Uncomfortable. I moved on. In a second bed, it seemed that whoever had slept there was too soft and mushy on the inside. Then I found a third bedroom, and the vibrations of life I got from that bed were perfect. Just right. I could have stayed there all day, waiting until the person who belonged to this room showed up. And I could stare into his or her eyes, stealing the life from them. Turning them into stone.

Is this what Tara had felt when she came into our house the first time?

I left the room and went down the stairs, knowing the family was down there.

"Daddy," I heard a child crying. "Somebody's been sitting in my chair. And now it's all broked up!"

"What happened to my pie?" I heard the mother call. "Someone's been at my pie!"

"Hey, who messed up the covers?" I heard someone else call upstairs. "I just made this bed! Who's been in it?"

They all began to move in my direction, but that was okay. I could have hidden again, but I wanted to be seen. I did have the good sense to slip on my sunglasses, though.

The father noticed me first. Then a little girl, who hurried to him, grasping on to his pant leg. The mother came in from the kitchen, and a kid a year or two older than me stopped on the stairs when he saw me.

"Who are you?" the father asked. "What are you doing here?"

I just smiled at him. At all of them. "Making myself at home," I told them. "And what a nice home, too."

My hunger was growing, taking me over. Turning Nasdaq and other small creatures to stone was like taking tiny tastes of a huge feast. My appetite was whetted, and now I had to have more.

"Get out!" the mother said, but didn't step any closer. "Get out or I'll call the police."

They could sense my power. They were afraid.

That's when my mind began to say things. Scary things. *I don't know them,* I began to tell myself. *If they turn to stone, so what? Why should I care? It's not like I'll ever see them again. It's not like I'll ever get caught.*

I shook my head, trying to chase these terrible thoughts away. How could I think such things? What was wrong with me? Before the voice of hunger began gnawing on my mind again, I left, moving at a speed only a Gorgon could. Running between the seconds. To those people, I probably seemed to vanish before their eyes, leaving them to wonder for the rest of their short mortal lives, *Who was that stranger sitting in my chair? Eating my pie? Sleeping in my bed?* Just some crazy kid with crazy locks, who saw us and ran away. That's all. They would never know how close they had come to their own stony ends.

I ran through their yard, across the street, and into the woods, finding that no matter how fast I ran, I never lost my breath. I knew the direction I was running in. I could sense direction just as I could sense life, and soon I came out of the woods to see my school up ahead, with the students already arriving. Just a few. Not the crowds that would be there in another half hour. Going to school seemed pointless to me now. School was for regular kids, who would grow, and get jobs, and die someday. But now I wondered, would I ever grow beyond fifteen? Was I stuck at this age for all eternity? That would really be a curse. Or perhaps, in the same way I could stretch and shrink the flow of time, could I change my age by merely thinking about it? I had so many questions, and I knew that the only one who could answer them was Tara. I didn't want to see her now. I felt so strange within my own skin, I didn't want to face her until I felt more comfortable, more *myself*, whatever that meant now.

Would she be at school today? Maybe, but I could deal with that. There were plenty of ways to avoid talking to her, if I really wanted to. Perhaps there was no longer a need for me to go to school, but I wanted to go there, anyway. I desperately wanted something normal back in my life, if only for a few hours. The hunger had faded just a bit now. I figured I could control the hunger in a familiar place, around people who I knew. I was sure of it.

I crossed beneath the stone arch of Excelsior Academy, telling myself that the reason I wanted to be there was simply to go to class. Funny how your own mind can trick you into believing things that just aren't true.

Hiding behind my sunglasses, I made my way right to the library. Even through the dark lenses, the people around me shone in dazzling color compared to the strange grayness of the walls and floors. I could smell them, too. Not their hair gel, or deodorant, or nasty gym smell, but some other smell. The smell of their life. I could hear myself groaning with hunger, so I picked up my pace, practically knocking the door to the library off its hinges as I entered.

"Parker Baer!" the librarian complained. "Control your impulses!"

"Sorry," I said, then grabbed some teen magazine and headed to the farthest table in the dimmest corner, away from any of the other kids. I forced myself to read articles about things I didn't really care about. According to my watch, there were still twenty minutes until my first class would begin. My first blissful distraction of the day. Who would have thought I'd ever call algebra blissful?

With no patience for waiting, I concentrated on my watch and the movement of time, until I could see the minute hand moving at the speed the second hand usually moved. Sounds around me became whiny and high-pitched. Perhaps it was this acceleration of time that kept me from noticing Danté sitting down beside me.

"Dude, I've been watching you. It's like you haven't breathed for a whole minute."

I turned to him slowly, time resuming its normal pace. "Leave me alone, Danté," I heard myself say, with a dead flatness to my voice.

He leaned forward, misreading the tone of my voice to mean something else. "I guess you heard, then."

"Heard what?"

"Ernest." He spoke in a whisper, like it was too terrible to speak out loud, which it was. "He's dead."

I just stared at Danté through my lenses, my jaw dropped open.

"I know, I can't believe it, either," said Danté. "But whatever strange disease he had, it killed him. Something to do with the hardening of his bones. It's like his bones just kept getting thicker, until everything else just got pushed out." Danté shivered. "Sick."

"That's not what happened," I told him.

"Why, what did you hear?"

"It's not what I heard; it's what I know. He petrified. He turned to stone."

"Hey, man, don't make jokes, okay? The dude is dead. It's not funny."

"And I've got news for you," I added. "There's going to be a whole lot more. I could even tell you who."

"Parker, you're really starting to freak me out," Danté said, leaning away. "I mean first the freaky hair and now all this freaky talk. That's freaky squared."

I understood now how Tara saw people. Like food. That's what I was beginning to see now. Even Danté. Remember that old cartoon: two guys stuck on a desert island, one guy looks at the other, and instead of seeing his bud, he sees a roast turkey? That's what it was like looking at Danté. It was probably the most disturbing thing I had ever felt.

I suddenly had an absolute *need* to turn something to stone, as overwhelming as the need to breathe. "I have to find something big," I said, more to myself than to him. "An elephant, a whale—anything!"

"Just when I thought you couldn't get any weirder . . . what are you gonna tell me next, you're a zombie that must eat human brains?"

I almost laughed. He had no idea how close he was.

Danté must have seen something unspeakable in my nasty little grin, because he stood up and backed away.

"I've had it with you, man. I don't know what's wrong with you, but you're in definite need of some major therapy."

He turned to leave, but I couldn't let him go like that. I just couldn't. If there was anyone I could spill my guts to, it was Danté. He might not believe me, he might call me crazy, but if I showed him how I could turn animals to stone, he'd have no choice but to accept it, and then maybe I'd have someone on my side. Someone besides Tara.

"Danté, wait!" I followed him out into the hall, moving so remarkably fast, everything was a blur. Suddenly I found myself in front of him, right in his path.

Danté just looked at me, stunned. To him, it must have seemed like I just appeared there. "How did you . . ."

"Never mind how," I told him. "There are other things we need to talk about."

I was about to tell him all about Tara, all about who she was and the cursed gift she had given to me, but instead of talking, I found myself reaching for my glasses and pulling them off my face. I couldn't stop myself.

It took only an instant for me to catch Danté's gaze in mine. Triggering the change in Danté wasn't as easy as it had been with the animals I had come across, but I was still able to do it.

I gasped a breath of deep relief. My curls squirmed, satisfied in a way they hadn't been when I had petrified animals. And suddenly I realized what I had done.

"Danté! Danté, I'm sorry! I'm so sorry!" But what did *sorry* mean now? His eyes were already starting to glaze. His skin had begun to pale.

"Your eyes," he said weakly. "Don't look at me again, okay? Just don't look at me." He turned and staggered away. Other kids were looking at me now, wondering what had happened and why Danté was acting so strangely. Quickly I put on my sunglasses, desperate not to catch anyone else's gaze, and I bolted from school.

How long would it take for Danté's flesh to turn? Weeks? Days? It didn't matter, because there was no stopping it. I had turned my best friend to stone.

17

▲

THE FIELD
OF DRAGONS

Danté was as good as dead. I could run as fast and as far as I
wanted, but I couldn't outrun that simple fact. I could hurl
myself off the highest cliff to purge myself of the guilt, but I
would merely walk away from it uninjured. This act of turning a
friend into stone was the final stage of my initiation into Tara's
dark world. I had become a Gorgon, like her sisters and her.
Hideous to behold. Ugly in a way beyond words. I understood
the myth now. It wasn't a physical ugliness, but an ugliness of
spirit. My spirit bore that same ugliness now.

I ran all the way home, but I had no intention of staying.
I would not face my parents, or my ailing brother and sister. I
headed straight for my room and began to pack. My gym bag
couldn't carry much, but I realized there was little I needed to
take with me. A few changes of clothes. A picture of my family. It's
funny how few "things" really matter, when you think about it.

I had no idea where I would go, but I didn't care. I was going
away. That's all that mattered. I had to get away from this place.

Away from people I knew—away from people, period. I could never again be in a place where I would be tempted to remove the shades that shielded my eyes and petrify another human being. Just because I couldn't resist it when faced with Danté didn't mean I couldn't teach myself to be stronger. Given enough time, I could learn to fight that urge, and now I had all the time in the world.

As I zipped my gym bag closed, mentally plotting my path out of town, I heard someone crying. It was a man. I focused my attention on the life energies around me, which I could sense like a scent. It was not within the house, but outside. Out back. I went downstairs and out the back door, to see my father, head in hands, sobbing on a chair beside the pool. Garrett stood next to him, just watching. I had never heard my father cry before—until now I had thought he only had two emotions: frustration and annoyance.

"Dad?" Checking to make sure my sunglasses were firmly in place, I slowly walked over to him. "Dad—what are you doing here? Shouldn't you be at work?"

"It's not a good day, Parker," he said through his tears. "It's not a good day at all."

Garrett, I noticed, said nothing to comfort him. He just stood there, looking down.

"Things like this shouldn't happen," Dad said, doing his best to hold back the flow of tears. "They don't happen. How could it happen to us?"

"What things?"

But it was like he wasn't hearing me, he was so lost in his own thoughts. "You spend your life working, providing for your family. You buy a big house; you give them everything they could possibly need. And *this* is what happens."

He threw a quick, pained glance at Garrett. And this time, when I looked at Garrett, I noticed something I should have noticed right away. Garrett wasn't moving. He wasn't shifting his weight from one foot to the other, like he always did. He wasn't looking at his watch; he was just standing there, staring at Dad. He was paler than ever before. The shade of his pale gray eyes was the exact shade of the color of his skin. I took a few steps closer; I touched his arm, his fingers. They were as cold and rigid as death.

"Garrett, no!"

There's a vein—you know the one. It runs along your wrist, winding up your arm. Kind of a strange purple-blue line. It's the one they take blood from at the doctor's office. I watched as this vein, the last sign of life left to Garrett, slowly began to fade from blue to the same gray that filled the rest of his body. What had begun in him weeks before was almost done. A few more minutes, and he'd be completely turned to stone.

"Now Katrina's come down with it," my father said. "Same symptoms." Then he turned to me. "Looks like we're going to have statues of all of you around the pool." He laughed bitterly at the awful thought, then put his head in his hands and cried once more.

Whatever else I had become, I was still human enough to feel my father's pain. After that, I couldn't just run away. Escape wouldn't be that easy for me, because I was still saddled with a conscience. Perhaps Tara had shed her conscience years ago, or maybe she had never had one, but I still did, and I was glad. It was the only thing that kept me human.

As I stood there watching my father mourn for my hardened brother, a sound came hissing over the tops of trees. It was far off, but my hearing was tuned beyond human capabilities. It was the sound of distant, labored grinding. Metal against metal. Gears and pistons painfully pumping in a forgotten, old oil field.

I left the pool, crossed the tennis court, and strode through the grass of our huge yard until I came to the woods that bordered our property. There was no path from here to the oil pumps, but I didn't need one. Their sound rang in my ears like evil church bells. It was Tara calling to me, I knew. I had the power to resist the call, but I didn't want to. I had to face her, although I had no idea what would happen when I did. She had destroyed all three of us Baer kids. My brother was stone, my sister would soon follow, and my curse was a fate worse than stone. I was immortal, with a hunger so uncontrollable I would destroy my own friends to satisfy it. I was strong in so many ways now, but that hunger was stronger than me.

I walked miles until I reached the abandoned road that led to the hidden oil field. Five of the six wells bobbed up and down, their rusty gears groaning in complaint. The insect eyes painted on their bulbous heads seemed to follow me as I entered the clearing. The sixth well was unmoving, the creature's "head" bowed low, as Tara repainted its face. This creature was not an insect anymore, but a dragon: a beast with menacing yellow eyes and razor-sharp fangs.

"Giving your friends a new look?"

She turned to me and smiled that warm, disarming smile that had always left me so defenseless. But I was wise enough now not to lower my defenses at all. I kept my distance and kept my face as cold as stone.

"They're wrong as insects," Tara said, putting down her paintbrush and slowly sauntering toward me. "Powerful predators are what they ought to be. Just like us."

"Just like you," I corrected.

"Are you still in denial, Parker? Do you still refuse to accept what you are?"

I didn't answer her.

"I can sense that you've turned your first human. Did you enjoy it, Baby Baer? Who was it? I want to know every wonderful detail."

She stood right in front of me now, and I refused to back away. She reached out and touched my long, twisting locks, but I reached up, grabbed her firmly by the wrist, and moved her hand away.

She looked at me, perhaps trying to read something behind my dark lenses. "Still mad at me, Parker? Still angry that I chose you for my most wonderful gift?"

"It's not a gift; it's a curse. It's horrible. You're horrible."

She tugged her wrist out of my hand. "Then so is every human being. You breed and murder animals to serve on your tables. You lure fish, then tear them out of the water and let them suffocate. You shoot birds and beasts for sport, and half the time you don't even eat them."

"That's different!"

"Why?"

"Because we don't kill our own kind!"

"And neither do we! You and I are not human anymore, Parker. We're something more. Something greater. Human beings are predators, plain and simple. And eventually every predator becomes prey."

There was truth to her argument. Brutal, maybe, but it was truth nonetheless. Humans were the most successful predators on earth. Not sharks, or tigers, but us puny, civilized humans. Her hand was in my hair again. This time I closed my eyes, enjoying the feeling.

"We are a new link in the food chain," she told me gently. "You mustn't feel guilty about that. . . ."

"But my family . . . my friends."

"Mourn for them," Tara said. "Mourn for your old life, but don't let it stop you from accepting your new one." Then she leaned forward and whispered, "I'm your only friend, Parker."

"I hate you," I whispered back.

"That will change," she said. "I want to give you something. One more gift." Then she reached into her pocket and pulled out a hunting knife, shiny and deadly sharp. I backed away.

"I've never done this for anyone before . . . but I'm doing it for you." Then she reached up, grabbed two of her shiniest curls, and with a grimace, she tore the knife through them.

I don't think I can describe the scream of pain that came out of her then. Not in the deepest torture chamber has such a scream ever been heard. It could have made stone shiver.

Tara fell to her knees, and the two locks wafted to the ground. They squirmed for a moment, then were still. As the hair died, it turned from gold to ashen gray.

"There," she said, her voice barely a whisper. "I've released your brother and sister."

I was speechless. My brother and sister were free? I reached to my own curls, thinking about Danté.

"Don't try it on yourself," she warned. "The pain would destroy you." She picked herself up, still weak from the experience. "But I was willing to experience that much pain for you."

She came over to me, already recovering from her pain.

"We will be wonderful together," she said. "We can go anywhere, do anything. We will be companions, Parker. Eternal companions."

I was repelled, yet drawn to the idea at the same time. Both feelings were so powerful, I felt I'd be torn apart.

"I know what you're feeling," Tara said. "Love and hate, terror and peace. To feel both extremes at once—that's our nature, Parker. All your life you've lived a lukewarm existence: never too warm, never too cold. That's not living. Now you will learn to live the extremes and embrace them." And she hugged me as she said it. It felt horribly wrong. It felt totally right. I now lived at the extremes.

"We are two of a kind," Tara said. "The only two."

Something about that didn't ring true. It took a moment until I realized why. "We're not the only two. What about your sisters?"

She took a step away. "My sisters are in a gallery at the Louvre," she said, with malice in her voice.

"What are you talking about?"

"They fought a thousand years ago and caught each other's gaze. They turned each other to stone. Now they're just two statues in a museum."

I stared at her in disbelief. "But . . . but I thought Gorgons were immortal."

To which she answered, "They are."

I didn't have time to think about what that might mean for her solidified sisters, because a sudden engine roared up behind me.

"Parker! Step away!" a male voice said, but before I could move, an angry gray slice of steel passed before my vision. It was a blade. A chain-saw blade. It came down inches away from me—but I quickly realized it wasn't meant for me—it was meant for Tara. She backed away in a flash, just missing the buzzing blade.

I turned to see Mike Fisher, the sculptor, wielding his chain saw like a broadsword.

"Sculptures with fingerprints? Reports of kids turning to stone? At first I thought there had to be another explanation, but no matter where I looked, it all kept coming back to you."

He swung the blade again but missed, because he wasn't looking at her. He couldn't risk that she'd take off her glasses and use her lethal gaze on him. "If I had any doubts, they're gone after what I just heard." He pulled the blade back for the next swing, and it came dangerously close to me.

"Move away, Parker," he said. "We both know what she is. We both know she has to be destroyed."

"You're crazy! She can't be killed!"

"There's one way to kill a Gorgon," he said. "If the myths are right, the only way to kill a Gorgon is to cut off its head."

Yes! He was right! The myths said that Perseus had done it—although now I knew that Perseus had never gotten his sword near her neck.

Tara seethed in this standoff against the artist. Her anger flared in her curling tendrils of hair, which now squirmed in fury.

"How could something as vile as you exist?" Mike said. "How many people have you destroyed? For how many years?"

"More than I can count for longer than I can remember," she said, and I knew it was not just a boast, it was true. The statuary of museums and palaces around the world must have been filled with her victims—not carved by the hands of men, but hardened by the eyes of a Gorgon. "You will be just one among thousands," she told the artist. "You'll die like Perseus, and I will spit on your cold stone face." She tore off her sunglasses and hurled them to the ground, but Mike turned his gaze downward, toward her feet, refusing to meet her gaze.

"Take off your glasses, Parker," she demanded. "He's got to look at one of us sooner or later."

I just shook my head.

"I said, 'Take off your glasses.'"

Mike seemed confused for a moment, until he took a good look at me. "She's made you like her! She's turned you into one, too!"

"Take off your glasses now." The command was almost impossible to resist—still, I fought the urge to obey and kept the glasses on.

She glared at me, but I knew better than to meet that gaze.

"You don't want to be like her," Mike said. "I know you don't. Death is better than that. Let me end it for you right now." Then he revved the chain saw.

Until that moment, I hadn't realized how unafraid of death I was. Perhaps because I now knew something worse than death. I had not bled when I had crashed from the cliff. Was I now completely like Tara? A bloodless creature of darkness? No. I would not be that monster.

Mike came straight for me. I didn't move, didn't flinch—but Tara stepped in front of me with supernatural speed. As the chain saw came down toward me, she grabbed Mike's hand, deflecting it. Then Tara tore the chain saw away from Mike and hurled it with such force that it disappeared over the trees. She grabbed him by the neck, lifting him from the ground. He tried to turn his eyes away, but couldn't. For a brief instant his eyes met hers, and that's all it took.

Tara had said that when you were angry enough, you could turn someone to stone in a matter of seconds. I watched in breathless disbelief as veins of gray spread out from his eyes, along the surface of his skin. His chest rose and fell once as he tried to scream, but then it solidified. His heart hardened. The artist petrified head to toe before my eyes. When the last bit of pink bleached from his fingertips, I knew it was done. Then Tara dropped him. He landed on his feet, but then tipped over like a felled tree, hitting the ground with such a heavy thud, the earth shook.

Tara scowled at me as I stared at the stone body of the artist. "You stupid, stupid boy," Tara said. "You would rather die than be my companion?"

I didn't answer her—I just stared down at the sculptor's petrified form. When I finally looked up at Tara, her glasses were back on.

"Don't you understand, Parker?" she said. "We're all we've got. You'll never be free of me, and I'll never be free of you."

She was right. As hard as it was to accept, she was right . . . and I knew what I had to do.

I stood up, turned to Tara, and dug within myself for the worst feeling I could muster. Hatred. Black, festering hatred. Hatred was the core of a Gorgon's power, and since I was now one myself, I knew I had that within me.

I pumped up from the deepest pit of my soul the most lethal of feelings, then I tore off my glasses and stared Tara in the eye.

She gasped and took a step away. "No!"

It was the first time I had ever caught her off guard.

I had drawn my weapon, and so she quickly drew hers in response; she pulled off her glasses, leaving us both staring into each other's horrible eyes.

There is no way to describe what I saw in her eyes. The myths of Medusa speak of an ugliness so overwhelming it transmuted flesh into stone. No one could survive the ugliness betrayed by those eyes.

Her fury was like molten lava: hot and horrible, stone in its most dangerous form. "I freed your brother and sister, and *this* is how you repay me?"

"You don't belong in this world," I told her. "And now neither do I." Whatever ugliness she had, I now had it, too, and knew I could match it. This moment did not call for a delicate, slow turning of flesh, but a sudden detonation, just as she had done to the artist. No eating of sand and drinking of milk, but a quick and devastating alchemistic transformation.

My hideous curls quivered as I forced the newfound bitterness of my soul through my eyes into hers, even as she did the same to me. Triggering her change was like trying to throw a heavy steel switch—the kind Dr. Frankenstein used to bring lightning down to his monster. I felt the weight of her resisting the change, but she had been weakened when she had cut those two curls from her head. A moment more, and I felt the change sweep through her like wildfire.

"You don't know what you've done!" I heard her say. "You don't know wh—" and then her words stopped. I tried to open my mouth, but could not. I no longer had the ability to speak— and I knew that what I had done to her, she had done to me as well. Just like her sisters had done, we had destroyed each other.

With my eyes fixed forward, locked on Tara's eyes, I watched her flesh turn gray, her eyes turn gray, and finally her tangle of twisted hair turn gray, from the roots to the very tips. I could feel it in myself as well. A growing numbness. My toes and fingers, my elbows and knees, everything locking in place, never to move again. I breathed in, then my breathing stopped. My heart stopped. I could feel nothing beneath my neck.

I awaited the moment of my death as the numbness spread up my neck, through my jaw, ears, and face, and finally along the thick strands of my own hair until I could feel nothing. Nothing at all. But where was death?

I held out for the release of my spirit from the stone vessel of my body, but the release never came. Then, with growing and terrible awareness, I realized the truth.

I was immortal.

I was solid stone, but still, I could not die.

Dimly, through my stone eyes, I could still see Tara's solid form in front of me, the expression of fury and shock still on her marbleized face. I could feel her spirit there, as trapped as mine, never to turn another person to stone. Never to look away from each other.

I had won! I had saved the world from the likes of her. Of *us*. My victory was all I had now, and so I savored it as best I could, as I stared into Tara's eyes.

And I'm staring still.

No one ever found us. No one ever comes to our hidden oil field, and I now measure time not by days, but by the passing years. The path to this place must have choked with weeds long ago, and if the night brings stars, I cannot see them, for all I see is her. Tara. My friend. My enemy. My victim and my destroyer— our eyes fused in a frozen gaze until the rains erode the stone of our bodies . . . until our hardened flesh is turned to sand and carried off, grain by grain, by the wind.